The Ripper's Daughter

by Pamela Turner

a BlackWyrm book
Louisville, Kentucky

THE RIPPER'S DAUGHTER

Copyright ©2014 by BlackWyrm Publishing

A BlackWyrm Book
BlackWyrm Publishing
10307 Chimney Ridge Ct, Louisville, KY 40299

Printed in the United States of America.

ISBN: 978-1-61318-162-1

Cover design by Dave Mattingly
Edited by Annie Rodriguez

First edition: March 2014

To James. Thanks for your support and love.

Chapter One

Rumors spread Jack the Ripper haunted the river city when a newsboy discovered the mangled remains of a prostitute in an alley in Louisville's Chute section.

"Think it's the Ripper, mate?" Francis poured a shot of brandy for a customer.

"Even if it was, there's not a thing I can do about it." I slung my white bar towel over one shoulder. My days as a Scotland Yard detective inspector had ended when I'd left London.

The Cloak and Dagger hummed with customers discussing the Spanish American War and the Boxer Rebellion. Pungent cigar smoke floated in a dirty white haze over the room accompanied by the stale smell of beer.

The door opened, and a young girl, no more than seven or eight, entered, carrying a growler. She handed the tin pail to Francis.

He filled the receptacle with beer. The girl reached into a patchwork pocket sewn on her dress, and pulled out a nickel. Stretching up on her toes, she placed the coin on the counter. Francis handed her the growler. She furrowed her brow in concentration as she wrapped her hands around the handle and pulled it toward herself.

The girl's progress to the door was slow and labored. Beer sloshed over the sides with each step, dripping foam and ale. The door opened, and a young woman stood aside to let her pass.

"Hello, Charlotte," I greeted.

"Hello, Nathan. Francis." Charlotte climbed onto a barstool, and placed her drawstring purse atop the counter. "Whiskey, please."

I poured her drink. Charlotte drained the amber liquor in one swallow.

"I suppose you've heard about the murder." She smoothed her gored skirt, and glanced at the *Courier-Journal* next to my elbow. Her face appeared strained under the gas lights; her brown eyes hollow and rimmed with dark circles, brunette hair falling in haphazard curls.

"Aye." I refreshed her whiskey.

"We're afraid to be alone." Charlotte curled her fingers around the shot glass. "The police don't bother with our lot." Bitterness tinged her voice.

"I'm sure they're doing their best."

Charlotte downed the second shot and set the glass atop the bar. She maintained a tenuous but distrustful relationship with the police as did most ladies of the night. They looked at her kind with jaundiced eyes, but a tacit agreement seemed reached by both sides. The ladies knew not to draw attention to themselves if they wanted to avoid arrest.

"Maybe Scotland Yard, but not here. We're expendable."

Before I could assure her the prostitutes in Whitechapel had also been considered disposable, Francis came over.

"What brings you here tonight?" he asked.

Charlotte gave him a stained-tooth smile. "A girl needs a drink to fortify her against the night and all that lurks in it now."

He gathered empty beer steins at the end of the bar. "Aye but if you let me take care of you..."

"Francis!" Charlotte's mouth fell open. I shrugged and turned my attention to a customer. I'd no interest in their flirting. They seemed to enjoy their playful conversation, which they often indulged in when Charlotte stopped in for her nightly shot or two. I knew better than to believe Francis's insistence that he only saw her as a friend. His face lit up whenever he saw her, but he understood money ruled her heart, not romance.

Francis looked out of place compared to the rest of this lot in here. His blue-gray eyes appeared large, almost owlish, behind wire-framed spectacles. Even his hair imitated tufts of the bird, blond and center-parted. Tall and lean, almost gangly, he seemed better suited for teaching or reporting than tending bar.

Most of my customers were poor and working class, rail and dock workers, whose lined, tanned faces showed the ravages of sun and wind, and whose rough, calloused hands promised hard, honest work.

Did the Ripper sit among them? For a moment, guilt gripped my conscience. If only I'd stopped him, my dear Grace might still be alive. She would torment me to the brink of insanity as a younger sister could and would do to her brother. The police never proved the Ripper killed her, but I couldn't help feeling she'd been one of his earlier victims.

Charlotte interrupted my thoughts. "The Christian Women's Temperance Union's planning another protest."

I dipped the pewter tankards into a bin of soapy water. The Temperance Union feared saloons, brothels, and gambling houses would entice youth down paths of sin and folly. Ironically, their censure only increased the curios to seek out such establishments, including mine, rather than stifle it. Spiritual warfare clashed with hedonism, and this recent murder could turn the battle in the temperance union's favor.

I wiped down the counter. "Francis, you don't mind closing?"

"No, Mr. James not at all." Despite the hierarchy of our respective positions, I preferred an informal atmosphere, having had enough of protocol working for the Yard.

I removed my apron, and hung it on the peg. "Good night, then." I reached for my derby and short frock coat. "Good night, Charlotte. Please be careful."

Charlotte gave me a defiant look, fist against a cocked hip. "I may be a woman, but I'm no weaker than you or him," she said as she pointed a finger at Francis and myself. "No matter what you men may believe." The teasing glint in her eye belied any complaint. Whether she'd admit it or not, she appreciated my concern.

I gave Charlotte what I hoped my most ingratiating smile. "Of course, lass. I had no doubts."

Outside, the air hung damp, heavy with the odors of oil, coal smoke, and steam from boats docked along the Ohio River Fourth Street wharf. Low clouds obscured the night sky. Lights from gas lamps flickered, haloing mist rising from cold cobblestones. Nearby, a woman's muffled laughter punctured the silence.

I continued southward. I covered my nose with my kerchief as the overpowering stench of dried dung and overfilled sewers assaulted my nose. My sense of smell was keener than most people, an asset at times, but a detriment at times like now.

A police whistle pierced the air. I stopped, trying to pinpoint the location.

There you go again. You're not a detective inspector anymore.

So why couldn't I resist the siren call of a possible crime?

Perhaps I'd made a mistake leaving Scotland Yard, but I just couldn't return. Not only had I failed to stop the Ripper, my former colleagues would never understand my sacrifice, what it had done to me personally – to my family.

Jack the Ripper wasn't human. His last victim, Mary Kelly, had been buried, and he'd vanished it appears into thin air by the time I realized the truth.

St. James Court loomed ahead, dominated by a bronze fountain of Venus, a reminder of the now-defunct Southern Exposition.

Stephen waited for me at the front door of our Queen Anne. He ushered me inside, taking my coat and hat.

"How was work tonight?" he asked, after hanging my outerwear in the hall closet.

The chesterfield cushion dipped as I sat. Stephen removed a decanter of brandy from the liquor cabinet. I needed a drink. This recent killing, and the possibility the Ripper roamed Louisville's streets, pinched my stomach with sharp, painful claws. "A prostitute's been murdered."

Stephen arched eyebrows above sapphire blue eyes as he handed me a snifter. "No doubt Sergeant Pierce will come by." He sat next to me, crossing long legs.

I balanced the glass atop my thigh and savored the warmth of his nearness. "Perhaps." After learning I'd been a DI, Sergeant Pierce, of the Louisville Police Department, often visited to seek advice on certain cases in an unofficial capacity.

"You aren't thinking of getting involved, are you?" Stephen's eyes darkened.

Chapter Two

Something primal stirred in me. A faint coppery smell triggered an ache in my fangs, which dropped in anticipation. I set the snifter on the coffee table.

Stephen locked the door, and pulled the brocade curtains closed. We needed to take precautions, lest someone see us.

Our neighbors had no idea vampires lived among them.

He returned to the sofa. Light from a gas lamp threw shadows across his saturnine face and slanted into an inverted "V" against the bridge of an aquiline nose. Despite shoulder-length dark hair, a fashion of dandies, he shared no other similarities in dress or mannerisms. Nor did he wear the uniform of a valet, but one that befitted his lineage, a double-breasted gray waistcoat with matching trousers and a white studded shirt.

Class meant nothing tonight. His carotid artery pulsed, calling me. I licked dry lips, desire pooling in my stomach, and shifted in my seat, impatient and eager to drink.

Stephen leaned his head back. Fingers trembling, I fumbled with his shirt studs, pushing aside the starched collar to reveal a pale throat. Leaning close, I breathed in the scent of sandalwood soap.

He made no sound as I licked salty skin, readying him. His fists clenched, and I placed my hand over them in a protective gesture.

Stephen closed his eyes. His sluggish heartbeat in sharp contrast to my rapid one.

I bit, aching fangs pricking flesh. Stephen tensed, arcing off the sofa, before relaxing.

A thin line of blood trickled down his neck. I lapped at it, and then began to drink.

His hand tightened on my knee. The first time, I worried I'd hurt him. He assured me the sensation was one of pleasure-pain, preferable to the discomfort he experienced when his body became gorged with too much blood. As a result, his heart struggled to pump the excess life fluid circulating through veins and arteries.

Why this happened to him and his kind, he never explained. I once asked Stephen what happened to vampires who never found companions like me. His glare convinced me to never ask again. Later, Stephen admitted those vampires either died of blood poisoning or were forced to resort to barbaric practices, like cutting.

I'd no idea about these complications when I first approached Stephen a decade ago to turn me into a vampire.

"Something bothers you." He stroked my hair.

I stopped drinking, and looked at him. Calm now, his eyes were closed as if I'd relieved him of a stressful burden. Somehow, during bloodlettings, he sensed my emotions. I hated that I was transparent, but glad I could confide in him without being ridiculed.

"Remember what I told you ten years ago?"

"You wanted to stop the Ripper."

I studied the pattern of blue veins along the back of my hand. "Francis asked if I thought the Ripper had come to Louisville. I hope I'm wrong, because if he has, the police won't be able to stop him. At least not without silver bullets."

Stephen nodded, seemingly unperturbed by my observation. "You doubt Sergeant Pierce will believe a wolf attacked the victim, much less a werewolf."

I leaned against him, listening to his steady heartbeat, glad fate had brought us together. "That's why I came to you. You were the only one who could help me stop him."

He wrapped his arm around me. "For your sake, I hope you never meet him."

For Grace's sake, I hope I did.

Chapter Three

He released me after a few minutes. Stephen removed a handkerchief from his pocket. He dabbed at the droplet of blood clinging to his throat like a glistening bead. The wound would heal within an hour, leaving no evidence of our encounter.

"Feel better?" I asked.

Stephen smiled. "Much." He stood and stretched, lengthening his lean body. "I think we could both use a drink." He poured two glasses of cognac. The liquor would wash away the blood's metallic taste.

He seemed healthier, if a little pale. His step was more energetic, eyes brighter.

I took my glass, and closed my eyes, inhaling the rich, wood smoke aroma. Stephen spared no expense buying the best liquor. He also purchased alcohol for The Cloak and Dagger.

The house, with its antique furnishings, and the saloon, belonged to Stephen. The tavern was a birthday gift, a means to earn money so I wouldn't feel obligated to him. Since becoming a vampire, I couldn't work certain jobs, especially ones requiring me to be in sunlight. It was possible to walk about in daytime under overcast skies but direct sunlight would have a devastating and possibly fatal outcome.

This irony carried over into our societal roles. Stephen's financial worth exceeded mine, yet he agreed to be my manservant. If it bothered him, he never let on that it did. Perhaps he preferred remaining in the background, drawing little or no attention.

"What are you thinking?" he asked.

"About us."

Stephen set his half-empty glass atop the side table. Putting an arm around my shoulders, he drew me close. I rested my head against his chest, listening to his heartbeat. Its beat had relaxed, pumping steadily, not as belabored as before I drank.

"You don't know how glad I am you came to me," he said, fingers tracing a path from my chest downward.

I closed my eyes. The recent consumption of blood, followed by cognac, and now Stephen's touch, conspired to lull me to sleep. This was much different from our first bloodletting. Recalling that time I frowned, remembering what he said afterwards. I remembered feeling dizzy when Stephen had drank from me. I blacked out. Awaking several hours later, I found myself lying on a brass bed. Stephen sat in a carved mahogany chair beside me. He looked worried. When I sat up, his concerned expression morphed into a hesitant smile. After confirming I was all right, he poured me a shot of whiskey.

He confessed, "You're the only one to survive the change." I hadn't realized there was a possibility that I wouldn't and I thought it was wise of him not to advise me of such. Perhaps my determination and motivation helped, although he suspected my biological and physiological makeup also played a role.

The murders suddenly stopped. My intention had been to use my newfound vampiric powers of speed, strength, and heightened senses to capture the Ripper. Faced with this cruel twist, I resigned my position, lest my associates discover my secret. London held too many unhappy memories for me. Stephen and I boarded a steamer for America. I realized I could never stay in England even though I didn't know what to expect.

It seemed law enforcement wasn't quite done with me even though I'd quit Scotland Yard. Once again Sergeant Robert Pierce visited me the next morning.

I'd started eating breakfast when Stephen announced the officer's arrival.

"Send him in." I couldn't help but smile at Pierce's unorthodox visits. He always seemed to know exactly when I took my meals. I took my coffee into the living room to meet with him.

Stephen returned a few minutes later with Sergeant Pierce. The officer wore his uniform. Aha, an official visit. He stood there holding his patrol cap in his hands.

"Good morning, Mr. James." He longingly gazed at my cup of coffee.

"Good morning, Sergeant Pierce. I take it this is not a social call." I gestured for him to take a seat. He remained standing. "Have time for coffee?"

"Thank you."

Ever the dutiful servant, Stephen poured the officer a cup from a silver coffee service.

Sergeant Pierce inclined his head. He stood, fingers wrapped around the handle, and seemed lost in thought.

"It tastes better if you drink it hot," I suggested.

"What?" Pierce looked confused for a moment. He shook his head, as if trying to clear his mind. "Yes, yes of course."

He wasn't usually this distracted. Something untoward must've happened.

"You didn't come here for coffee. So please tell me what is on your mind. What is the cause of this visit?"

Pierce's Adam's apple bobbed as he swallowed the hot liquid. He lowered the mug. "There was a murder last night. Quite a messy ordeal."

"Who?" I recalled the piercing shrill of the police whistle.

Sergeant Pierce tugged at his collar. Beads of sweat dotted his hairline. "You're not going to like this, sir, but she was a lady of the night." He gave me a sidelong glance. "I know you're kinder to them than most folks. Would you mind seeing if you can identify the body?"

"I don't know if I'll be any help. I don't really have ... what do you call it ... business. Yes that's the word I was looking for. I don't transact business with them."

Sergeant Pierce handed Stephen his cup. "Maybe not, sir, but I wouldn't feel right not to ask for your help." He held out his hand and we shook. "Good day, Mr. James. I'll see you in a couple of hours?" Not bothering to confirm, he turned to Stephen. "I can see my way out, thank you."

"You're not planning to go out this morning?" Stephen asked after Sergeant Pierce had left.

"He expects me."

Stephen gathered our coffee cups. "I don't like the risks." We'd made sure our house was protected from sunlight, having it built to our specifications. A covered verandah wrapped around the structure. The front door opened on the south side, so as to get the least amount of sunlight possible.

I followed Stephen into the kitchen. "I don't know why he insists on bothering you," he complained. He worked the hand pump, filling a large basin with water and soap flakes. "You're not a detective inspector anymore. You're done with it or at least that is what you keep saying," he said with an eyebrow arched inquisitively.

"No, but he thinks my expertise is worth seeking. So I will humor the chap and see if I can identify the woman." I had to admit being flattered.

Stephen slipped the breakfast dishes into the water. "You can't keep chasing your past forever."

I looked at him. Stephen had already rolled up his shirt sleeves and turned his attention to washing dishes, forearms glistening with water and soap.

"I wish you'd reconsider," he said.

"I'm only going to look at the body. I've no intention of becoming involved with the case," I said more to placate him than to justify why I really was going to go meet with him.

Stephen placed the last dish in the rack and dried his hands on a hand towel. Our lifestyle warned against us hiring servants. Stephen didn't seem to mind, but I couldn't help but feel guilty someone of his lineage was reduced to doing domestic chores suitable for a scullery maid.

He took my chin between his thumb and index finger, lifting my face to meet his. Soapy water dripped down his hand and onto his arm. "You're too kind-hearted for your own good." He leaned down, brushing his lips against mine.

I placed my arm around Stephen's waist and kissed him, my tongue exploring the corners of his mouth. He tasted like coffee and sugar.

Stephen began working the studs on my shirt. Skin prickled as my body temperature rose. He shifted the collar aside, and leaned in to gently bite at the juncture of my neck and shoulder.

He drank. His fangs sharp, mouth wet and hot against my flesh. My hands fisted against his back. "You're making me late..." I tried to sound stern, but it came out breathless and needy.

Stephen ignored me.

Knees weak, I sagged, needing to sit or lean against something. My head reeled as if from a lack of oxygen. Stephen guided me into the living room. He gently pushed me on the sofa and leaned over me. Brushing aside strands of my hair, he resumed drinking. Each pulse throbbed in counterpoint to his swallows. One hand reached down and kneaded my thigh muscle.

Pleasure threshold almost reached, I dug my fingers into his upper arms to help anchor myself against desire spiraling through me.

Stephen pulled back and wiped my blood from his lips, licking his fingers clean. "In case I don't see you again."

I kissed him. "I'll be fine."

He still didn't look convinced. I kissed him one more time before donning my derby and frock coat.

Outside, the overcast sky afforded me a degree of safety, but one I couldn't take for granted. Louisville weather was capricious at best. Cloud cover in one area could give way to clear skies a mile away.

I ran to board the mule trolley stopped across the street before it left without me. The driver shook the reins and shouted "Hie!" As the car jerked forward, I grasped the underside of the hard wood bench to avoid being unseated.

Thoughts raced through my head. What condition would the victim be in? Would I recognize her? Would I know her personally? The horrors visited upon Mary Kelly were forever etched in my memory. If this was the handiwork of the Ripper, the body would probably be unrecognizable.

Chapter Four

"There she is, sir. Sorry you have to see her like this." Sergeant Pierce gave me a sympathetic look.

The coroner lifted the sheet covering the remains of Louisville's latest murder victim. The woman's face was unmarred, eyes closed, dark lashes contrasting with pale skin.

Exsanguination was the likely cause of death, the disembowelment an afterthought. Vicious claw marks left bloody scars down her bare thighs.

My stomach heaved as I covered my nose and mouth to stem the rising queasiness. This murder fit the Ripper's modus operandi. The viciousness of the attack convinced me more than ever my elusive murderer had come here even though I had no proof he'd killed her.

"I don't know who she is," I admitted as I averted my face. The copper smell of her blood still assailed my nostrils. The coroner replaced the sheet. "She could be a recent arrival or just passing through the city. Poor woman." Steamboats stopped in Louisville on their way to Memphis and New Orleans. "If she's itinerant, it'll be harder to identify her."

Sergeant Pierce glanced at the body. "We'll circulate her picture, see if anyone recognizes her. Maybe we'll be lucky."

Luck. Many investigations had taken fortuitous turns, thanks to this twist of fate. Luck had helped me find wolf hairs at the Ripper's crime scenes. This bolstered my hypothesis Jack the Ripper wasn't human.

I jammed my derby atop my head. "Bring a picture to the bar. Maybe one of my regulars will recognize her. Good day, gentlemen." Before Sergeant Pierce could answer, ask more questions, or otherwise stall me, I hurried outside. The stench of the woman's dried blood was becoming too much. I was in danger of my fangs dropping.

***

Ten minutes later, I pushed open the door to The Cloak and Dagger. My bloodlust had subsided. The smell of another's could trigger a blood thirst although I only drank Stephen's blood. Stephen had warned instead of turning someone, I would most likely kill them.

"You don't look good, sir." Francis eyed me as he poured me a jigger of brandy which I downed in one gulp.

"Murder." I pushed the shot glass toward him. Francis obliged and poured another. "Sergeant Pierce thinks she's a prostitute." I looked over Francis's shoulder. "Is Charlotte here?"

Francis snorted. "Charlotte awake before noon? Are we talking about the same Charlotte?" He fell silent, expression serious. "How did she die?"

"Stabbed and mauled."

A look of consternation crossed his face. "Is it similar to the Ripper's?"

"Yes." I set the shot glass on the counter. I raised my hand to indicate I didn't need another. Francis put the whiskey bottle back on the shelf. "I hope I'm wrong, but I don't think so."

A customer approached the bar. I said, "Goodbye. I will be back later tonight." He gave me a distracted wave.

Outside, the late morning air warned of impending rain. I hoped Charlotte had found a warm, safe place to sleep. The mysterious woman's face appeared in my mind. I shuddered and was quite thankful that it wasn't our dear Charlotte lying on that table. Remorse overcame me.

Early in my law enforcement career, a murdered body filled me with anger and frustration. Anger someone had played God with another's life, frustration that finding the killer often proved difficult, if not impossible. I was disappointing the victims and their families besides letting down my fellow Scotland Yard colleagues.

Nightmares haunted me. I dreamt I was walking through a cemetery for months after encountering my first murder victim. Statues of weeping angels glared as I passed, their eyes accusing. Each face was that of the murdered woman.

Back home, I recounted my visit to the morgue.

Like Francis, Stephen inquired if the killing fit the Ripper's style.

"Unfortunately, yes." I wanted to be wrong.

"What do you plan to do?"

"I don't know." Strange how I'd prepared for this day. I wished it were a nightmare now that it might be here.

I retreated to my study after asking Stephen to bring me a cup of coffee and a sandwich. I pulled the much handled papers from a small cabinet. These were copies of the Ripper murder reports, news clippings, notes, sketches, and biographies of the victims. I spread them across my desk.

A letter fluttered to the floor, and I bent to retrieve it. A Cambridge address was scrawled across the cream-colored envelope in feminine cursive. It was the last letter I received from Grace while attending the university.

If only I'd come to London immediately after receiving her missive. I might've saved her life.

The best I could do now was avenge her memory.

I studied my notes for half an hour, searching for a motive, a possible clue to the Ripper's identity. Not that there hadn't been ample speculation. No one seemed safe, not even a Jewish butcher or member of the royal family.

These hypotheses seemed plausible but doubtful. I struggled to piece together a composite sketch. Words like "tall," "dark," and "powerful," were used to describe him, but such descriptions were useless. Many criminals fitted one or more of those portrayals.

A rap on the door brought me out of my reverie. "Come in!"

Stephen entered, carrying a tray with coffee and a roast beef sandwich. He pushed aside a pile of papers, and set the tray on the end of the desk. He glanced at my notes. "Any luck?"

"None."

"He may have changed tactics."

"Possible, but I don't believe so. He's succeeded in avoiding capture this far. No doubt, he believes he's invincible. And, as a wolf shifter, he also has the advantage of keen senses and a hunting instinct." I bit into my sandwich, brushing crumbs off the papers with a flick of my wrist.

Stephen leaned against the door. "You should get some sleep."

I shook my head. "I'll be all right." Apparently, Stephen remembered the earlier days, when I'd obsessed over the Ripper case, allowing lack of sleep, hunger, frustration, and anger to result in my throwing all of my research into the fire.

Luckily, Stephen had snatched the notes from the flames, saving hours of valuable work. He suffered second-degree burns on his hands. They healed within a day, another advantage of vampirism: I vowed never to make him go through that pain again.

Stephen was right. I needed sleep. I'd been awake nearly twenty-four hours, but had hardly noticed. Unlike ordinary humans, I could subsist on little sleep or food. Even a vampire has his limits, though, especially one who was as "young" as I. Lack of sleep was also detrimental to an investigator's mental state. It was important for me to have rest especially since I promised to relieve Francis from his shift at The Cloak and Dagger.

Opening the tavern hadn't been a spurious decision. They were excellent places to learn information. People might balk at talking with the police or a reporter. Tongues loosened by alcohol often wagged freely, sharing information they wouldn't share otherwise, if one paid attention.

"All right." I started to gather my papers, but Stephen gave me a warning look. He opened the door, knowing it was futile to argue with me any further.

I followed him into the hallway and upstairs to my bedroom.

Stephen turned down the comforter on the brass bed. "I'll call you when dinner is ready," he said.

I sat on the mattress and removed my shoes. "You'll let me know if Francis calls or Sergeant Pierce stops by again."

"If Sergeant Pierce does stop by, what would you like me to tell him?"

"That I'll be down in a moment." I pulled the cover over me, crossing my arms behind my head on the pillow.

"Knowing him, he'll show up around supper. I'll set an extra plate, just in case."

I couldn't resist an amused laugh at Stephen's adroit observation. Sergeant Pierce was a bachelor and probably didn't have anyone to cook for him. He'd once tasted Stephen's fried chicken, and insisted if Stephen were a woman, he might very well steal him away.

I'd never forget the horrified look on Stephen's face. Luckily, Pierce never saw it, and no one spoke of the incident since.

It was several weeks before Stephen made fried chicken again.

I closed my eyes, allowing myself to relax. Often, I found releasing vexing thoughts helped me find solutions I might not have considered otherwise. For example, someone using a pick axe to poke a chink in the dam of my brain, a previously trapped thought managed to leak through and into my conscious thought process.

No one knew what the Ripper looked like except of course his murder victims, and they couldn't talk. But why would the Ripper come here? Why not cities like Chicago, New York, or San Francisco, places with larger populations, where he could easily blend in and not be noticed? Louisville, a city of respectable size, hardly seemed a place important enough to attract the Ripper's attention.

Unless he was traveling by steamboat. But where to next? Up river or down river? I made a mental note to discuss my theory with Sergeant Pierce. Yawning, I closed my eyes. The pillow was cool against the back of my neck. That, along with the hissing of the gas lamp, soon lulled me to sleep.

How long I slept, I'd no idea. The room was considerably darker when I woke.

My door was open. Stephen poured a pitcher of water into the basin on the washstand.

"Supper's ready. Pork chops and corn pudding."

I sat up, stifling a yawn. "Any visitors?"

"No, sir." Stephen started to leave, but stopped on the threshold. "I called Francis to ask him to buy a newspaper just in case the murder is mentioned. He said it'll be waiting for you."

I looked up from lacing my shoes. "Well done. You'll make an investigator yet." I enjoyed teasing Stephen. For someone not interested in police work, he often thought like a detective.

I'd no idea if Stephen had ever worked. He'd been born into his role as a master vampire like others of his kin. Over the centuries, his family had accumulated great wealth, investing in stocks, real estate, and commodities. Stephen's overall net worth was probably more than the city budget.

We both lived what we hoped appeared as a respectable salary for a tavern owner. The house was our greatest expense, but a necessary one. Still, our Queen Anne paled next to the recently completed "Conrad's Castle," a limestone manor at the corner of St. James Court owned by Theophilus Conrad, a leather manufacturer.

Stephen left the room. Yawning, I shuffled to the washstand, and splashed water on my face. I hoped to stave off another face-splitting yawn, but failed. That was the insidious thing about naps. They only gave temporary relief.

***

I'd just took off my coat and hat to hang up at The Cloak and Dagger when Francis handed me the *Courier-Journal*. A small headline in the bottom right corner preceded a brief article about a young, unidentified woman who'd died under mysterious circumstances. A grainy picture accompanied the piece, and a caption encouraged anyone who knew her to contact the police.

Mysterious death. I resisted the urge to laugh. How euphemistic.

I folded the paper so the article faced upward. "Has Charlotte stopped by?"

"Not yet." Francis hung the bar towel on its rack. "If I see her on my way home, do you want me to tell her you're looking for her?"

"Yes, please. Sergeant Pierce also wants to see her." Seeing Francis's look of consternation, I quickly dispelled his fears. "Only to see if she can help identify the young woman in the newspaper."

He looked relieved. "If I see her, I'll let her know."

"Thank you." I donned my bartender's apron. The bar was doing a brisk business tonight. Discussion revolved around the murder victim, with customers emphasizing their opinions with jabs of their cigars.

The door banged open. All heads turned to see who was causing such a racket. A tall, broad-shouldered man strode past the tables, boots clomping on the hardwood floor. Dust motes swirled in his wake. The bar became rather quiet.

"What will you be having, sir?" I asked. A malevolent aura emanated from him, drawing icy fingers across my nape. I steeled myself, trying not to shiver.

He gave me a hard stare with intense, almost black eyes. "Whiskey." His voice was rough, as if he sandpapered his vocal chords.

I poured him a shot. His large square hand wrapped around the glass, and he drank. The jigger was probably no more than a drop given his size. His nostrils flared as he slammed the glass on the counter. A cruel smile tugged at his mouth. "Another." The crowd slowly went back to their business of drinking and speculating when they realized he just wanted to drink. They did it quietly though.

He pushed the glass toward me after his third shot and wiped his mouth with his coat sleeve. We stared at each other for a few seconds. His eyes gleamed with a maniacal light. For a brief moment, I swore I'd seen him before. He gave me a cruel smile, as if challenging me to order him to pay.

I'd rather lose money than have him continue to cast a pall over my establishment. "On the house, sir."

He nodded, turned, and strode out just as he strode in earlier. The room seemed to exhale a sigh of relief As soon as the door closed behind him.

I placed the shot glass in a bin of soapy water. I'd no intention of risking my customers' health after the outbreaks of cholera and typhus. My concern was also personal. I'd lost two brothers in infancy to a typhoid outbreak.

When the door banged open again, everyone in the tavern, including me, jumped.

Chapter Five

Charlotte looked around the room, hands on her hips. "What's wrong?" She jabbed me in the chest with an index finger. "You're white as a sheet. Looks like you've seen a ghost!"

I couldn't tell her why the man's presence unnerved me. Perhaps it was his powerful aura and commanding presence. Even more disturbing, though, was this sense of something smoldering beneath the surface, something I couldn't pinpoint, but enough to have chilled my blood.

"Maybe I have. Maybe I have." My voice drifting off, I quickly changed the subject. "Did you see Francis tonight?"

Charlotte sat on a barstool, long skirts and petticoats falling around her booted feet. "No." She smoothed her hair. "We did hear there was another murder."

I poured a shot of brandy. "Do you know her?" I placed my index finger on the small photograph, and turned the *Courier-Journal* toward her.

Charlotte sipped her brandy as she studied the picture. "She isn't one of Edna's girls. She doesn't look familiar at all. Big Edna hasn't taken on any new girls lately. Maybe she came from Lexington or Cincinnati."

I replenished her drink. She'd a valid point. I needed to ask Sergeant Pierce if he'd contacted police departments in the surrounding cities regarding missing girls or murdered prostitutes. "What will you do?"

She rested her elbows on the counter. "There's safety in numbers. Big Edna wants us sticking together. Watching each other's back if you know what I mean. Some are staying home safe and sound until the killer's caught."

I wanted to assure her the police had the situation under control, but she wouldn't believe me. "Maybe you should stay home as well, lass."

Charlotte laughed. "And who would pay my rent?"

"Aye, lass, you know who would do that."

Charlotte ignored me and continued to leaf through the newspaper. "Are you going to her funeral?"

"I'm not sure." It would be too painful. I hadn't attended Grace's; had no idea where she was buried. This young woman's funeral would only make me regret betraying my little sister even more. I needed to concentrate on finding the Ripper, whom I was positive had murdered both women.

"I'm going." Charlotte reached for a napkin and dabbed at the condensation ring her glass left behind on the bar. "Even if I didn't know her. It's my duty. She was one of us." She propped her jaw against her fist. "You'll attend my funeral, won't you?"

"You'll live a long time. This bar will probably be razed, and you'll still be alive."

"What about you? How long do you plan to live?"

I couldn't tell her the truth. "Long as possible."

A young boy, about five or six years old, entered the bar. He lugged a tin pail, fists curled under his chin.

Charlotte reached down to help him. The boy stared at her for several seconds before relinquishing the growler. She handed me the pail.

The boy scrambled atop a barstool and placed a nickel on the counter.

I filled the pail with beer. The boy reached for it. I shook my head. Dark circles under his eyes, pale face, and thin frame indicated he'd either recently been ill or hadn't eaten in a while. "You can't carry this." I turned to Charlotte. "Will you watch the bar until I get back?"

"Of course."

"Thank you, sir." The boy's voice sounded reedy. He slid off the barstool.

I lifted the pail. Despite its weight, I carried it without effort. The boy seemed impressed, staring at me with wide eyes.

"You're very strong, sir."

"Years of hard work." It wasn't an exaggeration. During my Scotland Yard years, I'd lifted corpses, helped right overturned carriages, and hauled all manner of debris.

He led me down cobblestone streets. Beneath the yellow glow of hissing gas lamps, women and men watched us as we passed. I ignored them, sensing suspicion more than malice. Only fair since I was a trespasser in their territory.

We drew close to the Market Street tenements. Here, night air was punctured by angry, drunken shouts and high-pitched screams. Two teenage boys ran past, almost bumping into me and upsetting the beer. My young escort ignored them, already inured to this life of violence and poverty.

A seedy-looking shotgun house anchored a row of similar houses at the end of the block. A haggard-looking woman sat on the stoop. She stood once she saw us approaching and wiped her hands on a threadbare dress.

"Where've you been, Robert?" She looked at me with distrustful eyes. Two of her front teeth were missing, from bad nutrition, abuse, or a fight. She hadn't bathed recently. She might've been pretty once, but years of ill-living had etched worry lines and a permanent frown on her aged face.

"At the saloon, like you wanted, Mother." Robert sat on the stoop next to a rusting wrought iron porch rail.

I handed her the growler. "It was too heavy for him, ma'am."

The woman continued giving me a suspicious look as she took the pail. "I suppose you'll charge extra." She set the growler down and reached into her dress pocket, pulling out a tattered leather coin purse.

I held up my hand. "No, ma'am. Always happy to help a customer. I'm Nathan James, owner of The Cloak and Dagger."

"Pleased to meet you, sir. My name's Rachel." The women slowly returned the purse to her pocket, as if expecting me to snatch it away. She glanced at Robert. "I wouldn't have sent him, except his lazy trollop of a sister's disappeared."

My detective persona raised its head in anticipation. "Missing, ma'am?"

Her distrustful look was probably permanent and not a result of my presence. "Aye. What do you care? You ain't a cop or one of those reporters, are you?"

"No, but a young woman was recently murdered."

Rachel gave a disdainful wave of her hand. "We heard 'bout that one. Not a local girl. Seen her walking around wi' some gentleman type. Tall, big guy dressed in black." She indicated his height with her arm, stretching it above her short frame.

The night air suddenly became more chilled, stirring hairs on my nape. Could she mean my mysterious visitor? "You've seen them?"

Rachel nodded, greasy strands of hair plastered against her neck. People like her generally avoided the police, viewing them with suspicion. If she gave me information I could take to Sergeant Pierce, it'd be worth my time coming here. "They walk about ne'er speaking to no one. Figured they come off one of them steamboats. A week later, he's walkin' around by hisself." She paused. "That 'twas the other day."

"How long has your daughter been missing?"

"'Bout a week, give or take a day or two. 'Course, she's been known to stay out to the wee hours. But she usually comes home." Resentment tinged her voice. "Thinks she's better than the rest of us."

"Can you think of anywhere she might have gone? Have you told the police?"

Rachel glared at me. "What would I be askin' police for? As for where she's got to, how the hell do I know? She keeps to herself most times. Don't bother me 'n I don't bother her."

I looked at Robert. His chin had dropped to his chest, eyes closed. From the slow, regular breathing, I presumed he was asleep or nearly so. Did he miss his sister?

"Can you describe her?" I crossed my fingers Rachel's description didn't fit the girl in the morgue. I'd no desire to report bad news.

She shrugged. "Dark hair. Blue eyes." She paused, pursing her lips. "Or were they green?" Another shrug. "Skinny. Tall."

"Her name?"

"Rosie. Short for Roseanne."

The chances of finding a tall, skinny girl named Rosie with dark hair and either blue or green eyes in a city with a population of 161,000 was nearly impossible.

I told Rachel I'd do what I could. Not that she believed me. Life for people like her and Robert, even the elusive Rosie, mocked them with empty promises. They'd probably moved to Louisville from a small town or the country, hoping to escape a life of poverty. Instead, fate had saddled them with bad luck, and no possible way out of it.

Music and rousting cheers greeted me when I entered The Cloak and Dagger. The applause wasn't for me, but rather for Charlotte, who played and sang a bawdy beer song on the upright piano.

I returned to the bar. Song finished, Charlotte joined me, blowing kisses to customers, who stamped their feet and yelled for more.

"Did you see the boy home?" she asked.

"Yes." I needn't tell her of his living situation. Perhaps that was what had drawn me to Charlotte – our shared childhood poverty. Growing up in Whitechapel with an alcoholic father, I'd supplemented our meager income by working as a pickpocket. I practiced on drunks first before moving into London's wealthier districts. There, I moved among crowds, dipping my hand into purses left carelessly open.

During my adolescence, dandies, young men with slim figures, longish hair and ruffled shirts, intrigued me. Said to emulate Oscar Wilde, they affected airs of world weariness and held lengthy conversations about art and literature at sidewalk cafes.

I experienced my first sexual stirrings, and understood who I was when I spied two of them kissing in the public bath.

I dreamt of those young men. I wondered what it would feel like. I kept my sexual encounters to myself, afraid of what would happen if anyone found out. Sodomy was against the law in England, and I'd no desire to be arrested.

Instead, I found myself handcuffed when I tried to hoist a wallet from Detective Sergeant Michael Albertson.

I was sentenced to the workhouse. DS Albertson talked with the judge and his superior at Scotland Yard. I was one of the lucky ones. They agreed to have me transferred into his custody. He became my family, my parents and sister having since died. He influenced me to join Scotland Yard a few years later.

While memories were nice to relive, it was near closing time. I gave last call then made the rounds, collecting empty mugs and plates.

Charlotte remained, even after the last customer had gone, to my surprise. She fingered the hem of her skirt. "Would you care to walk me home tonight?"

This was unexpected. "Are you sure?"

She nodded, dark circles under her eyes contrasting with a pale face. Whether she admitted it or not, these murders left her scared.

"I can't stay." I paused, hoping she understood the implication. "What about your clients?"

"I'm taking your advice. A day or two off." Charlotte stepped off the barstool. "If it's true there's someone killing us, I'd rather be safe than sorry."

"I'm glad you're going to take my advice, lass. I hate to think something might happen to you." I turned the chairs upside down atop the tables. "If you'll start sweeping, we'll be out of here sooner."

She grabbed the broom. I returned to the bar to wash the dishes.

"You never seemed the type of person to be afraid," I remarked, hanging bar towels on the rack.

"I never used to be," she admitted. "We get more hassle from the temperance unions than anyone else. But you worked on the Ripper case, you know what can happen." She stopped sweeping. "Do you think he's here?"

"I hope not." I traded my apron for my coat and hat. "Ready?"

Charlotte nodded. I turned off the gas lights. We stepped outside, and I locked the door.

Someone was watching us. I drew closer to Charlotte, and looked around, but saw nothing.

I offered her my arm. A swollen breast brushed against my bicep, and she gave me a coy look from under long, dark lashes.

I shifted my position.

Unfazed, Charlotte faced forward, a determined look on her face. I cringed inwardly. This escort idea was merely a ploy. She didn't feel safe going home with strangers, so she chose me. If she had her way, Francis would be the one escorting her home not me.

We took a mule tram to Green Street. This area was famous for its "disorderly houses." I recognized Big Edna's house, with its wrap-around verandah and gingerbread trim.

I accompanied Charlotte to the front door. Young, voluptuous women sat in cane rockers on the porch. They stretched lithe bodies, vying for my attention.

Charlotte ignored them. "Come inside for a drink." She pushed open an ornate, wrought iron and glass-paneled door.

"I need to get back." I lifted her hand to my lips and kissed it. More for the benefit of her and the ladies than for me. "Thank you for a delightful time."

Walking away, I couldn't help but cringe at the high-pitched laughter following me. But whether the women were laughing at me or Charlotte, I'd no idea.

Chapter Six

"You're late." Stephen took my coat and hat.

"I escorted Charlotte home."

He paused on his way to the closet, coat draped over his forearm. "A bit forward, don't you think?"

When he returned to the living room, I put my arms around his neck and kissed him. "She's worried about this recent murder." I grinned. "Besides, she likes Francis."

He gave me a disbelieving look.

I put my arm around his waist and drew him to the chesterfield. Two glasses of cabernet sauvignon waited on the coffee table. The burgundy color of wine stirred that longing for blood and Stephen in me. The wine tasted slightly bitter with a hint of chocolate. I savored the flavors, letting them roll across my tongue.

Stephen watched me, wine glass raised to his lips. He didn't swallow. Instead, he lowered the glass slowly, his eyes hooded. I set my glass aside, desire filling me. Perhaps it was the wine, or maybe the need to forget tonight's episode with Charlotte. I undid my shirt collar.

"Drink my blood."

A strange light came into Stephen's eyes. His fingers moved toward my throat, pressing against the carotid artery. I closed my eyes. I listened to his heartbeat and rush of blood through his veins.

He pinned me against the cushion, stretching his long frame over mine. Kissing my temple, he moved down to press small kisses to my cheek, jaw, and throat.

Pleasurable feelings rushed through me as Stephen bit.

A couple minutes later, he pulled back, wiping blood from his mouth. I stared at him, unable to look away from his neck. A deep, unquenchable hunger filled me. My fangs dropped, and I leaned in and punctured his flesh.

Blood flowed into my mouth, warm and coppery, sweeter than bitter wine.

Stephen pulled me against him and kissed the top of my head. "Something's bothering you."

He let me finish, not demanding an immediate response. I stopped drinking, and leaned against the cushion. "Things have become strange," I admitted, and told him about Rosie and the tall man.

"Rosie's mother could be right. The dead girl and your mysterious man could've come on one of the steamboats."

"I wonder if it was the same man who came into the tavern." I shuddered, remembering the negative aura surrounding my visitor. "Upset the customers, myself included."

"You don't think it was him, do you?" Stephen caressed my arm. I shivered with pleasure.

"I don't know." A tiny voice in the back of my mind accused me of lying, of not wanting to admit the truth. "What if Rosie's with the Ripper? She could be in danger."

"You intend to look for her."

"I intend to mention it to Sergeant Pierce." I stood and paced the room. "I tried to stop the Ripper and failed. I don't intend to let that happen again."

"What if he leaves before you get the chance or he's already gone?"

I shook my head. "I don't think he's left. Not yet. He came here for a reason. Question is why."

Stephen leaned back, fingers clasped behind his head. "Maybe he knows you're here, and wants to silence you."

I shuddered. A cold and unnerving sensation overcame me, as if the corpse of one of the Ripper's victims had touched the back of my neck with a skeletal hand.

Was the Ripper taunting me?

***

The next day, against Stephen's wishes, I readied myself to visit Sergeant Pierce.

"You're taking too many chances," he protested.

"Do I have a choice? Sergeant Pierce works the day shift." Luckily, the weather had remained dreary these past few days. I appreciated Stephen's concern. I was risking my life for a stranger. But Charlotte was a friend, and if I could stop the Ripper before she became a victim, it'd be worth it.

I'd phoned Sergeant Pierce at the police station, and he invited me to discuss the case over lunch. Knowing his intention, I offered to pay for our meal at The Cloak and Dagger.

"You said you had some news for me," Sergeant Pierce said, as we feasted on our meal of beer and roast beef sandwiches.

"Anyone report a missing young woman named Rosie?"

He shook open his napkin. "Can't say anyone has."

"She disappeared about a week ago, shortly after our unfortunate victim was killed." I swallowed a mouthful of beer, wiping foam from my mouth. "I've been asking around, but no one recognizes her. Not only that, she was seen in the company of our mysterious stranger."

"Doesn't mean she's connected to the murders, if that's what you're thinking," Sergeant Pierce opined. "If she's an adult, she can do what she likes, as long as it is within the law."

"Perhaps." I bit into my sandwich. "Rosie could be in danger if he's connected with the murders."

Like Stephen, Sergeant Pierce looked unconvinced. "You seem to think you have to protect every woman in the city, Nathan. It's not possible. Most likely this Rosie ran away. You know how these young people are nowadays."

"It's possible," I agreed, "but I don't think so." I decided not to tell him my concern stemmed from failing to protect my sister. Maybe it was misplaced chivalry or guilt, but I had to atone somehow.

Sergeant Pierce leaned back and raised his mug. "Why?"

"Her little brother, Robert. He came to the bar to buy beer for his mother, Rachel. I got the impression from her Rosie usually bought the beer. He didn't look well. Frail. And Rachel didn't look any better." I paused, remembering her weary expression, one that came from living in dire conditions. "Then again, I doubt she could walk a block without collapsing."

Sergeant Pierce talked with his mouth open, spewing crumbs on the tabletop. "But why hasn't she reported Rosie missing?"

"You know how people in the tenements feel about the police," I reminded him. "She probably assumes Rosie will come back or she's gone, run away, or dead. One less mouth to feed."

He pushed his empty plate to the center of the table, and pulled out a notepad and pencil. "Did she give you a description?"

"Unfortunately, it wasn't very good. Dark hair, blue or green eyes, thin and tall."

Sergeant Pierce scribbled notes before seeming to realize the futility of it. "Oh, hell!" He slammed the notepad on the table. "You've described a good number of young women in this city, poor or otherwise. How in God's name do you expect me or my men to find someone like that?"

I refrained from mentioning Scotland Yard had had an even less helpful description of Jack the Ripper.

"If I find any more information, I'll tell you," I promised.

Sergeant Pierce gave me a stern look. "Don't put yourself in any danger." He emphasized his remark by gesturing at me with his mug.

"Of course not." I changed the subject. "Have you discovered the identity of that young woman?"

"No. No one's come forward. It's as if she dropped out of thin air." Sergeant Pierce finished his beer, and lowered his empty tankard. "It's rather vexing. If we knew anything about her, we might be able to determine why she was killed or better yet who killed her."

"Any fingerprints?"

"Our killer's too clever. Must've worn gloves." He leaned back in his chair, draping his arm across the back. "We even tried asking the ladies of the night, but they've made themselves scarce. And the ones we talked to denied knowing anything."

I considered telling him claw marks didn't leave prints, but saw no need to rankle him. Instead, I drained my beer and held my mug aloft.

Francis came over. "Another beer?"

Sergeant Pierce shook his head. "I should be getting back to work." He tipped his cap to me. "Thank you for the hospitality."

"Did you learn anything new?" Francis asked, after the officer left. He collected the plates, flatware, and Pierce's mug.

I followed him to the bar. He placed the empty dishes on the sideboard.

"At this point, I think I know more than he does." I donned my coat. "Have you heard of a young woman named Rosie?" I gave him the skeletal description.

"Can't say I have."

"I can't help but wonder if there isn't a connection between our victim and the missing girl."

"You don't think they're the same person?"

"No. She doesn't fit Rosie's description." I reached for my derby. "I should check out the wharf." If the Ripper and the mysterious woman had arrived by steamboat, maybe a dock worker had seen one or both of them.

Outside, a bicycle whizzed past me toward the Chute neighborhood, rider peddling furiously. I jumped back, cursing.

The Fourth Street wharf was abuzz with activity. Sidewheelers and sternwheelers floated on the Ohio River, docked in their berths. Dock hands loaded and unloaded cargo while passengers watched. Steam, oil, and smoke created dark accents against the overcast sky.

I approached a dock worker, who glared at me as he hoisted a rope, gloves stained black with grease. "Can't you see I'm busy?" he snapped.

Undeterred, I pulled out the clipping of the young woman, and showed it to him. "Have you seen her?"

He gave the photo a cursory glance. "No."

"She may have come by steamboat." I glanced at the name painted in gilded letters on the side, "*The Memphis Lady*." A small sternwheeler with a length of about 150 feet. Not big enough to be called a "Queen."

The dock worker shrugged, never pausing as he coiled the rope. "Maybe she did, but not on this boat. Try somewhere else."

My efforts proved futile. If any dockhands had seen the mysterious woman, they didn't work on any of the steamboats here. Apparently, it'd sailed, leaving behind one, or possibly two passengers.

Disappointed with my efforts, I waited with the dock workers and passengers for a mule tram. The clatter of approaching wagon wheels was interrupted by the shriek of police whistles. The piercing shrills came from the direction of the Chute.

Once again, I couldn't resist the lure of a possible crime, and ran off to see what'd happened.

Vampirism has many advantages, including strength and speed. I could run without tiring and soon found myself standing before a bawdy house.

A small crowd had gathered, gawking at the eviscerated, bloody corpse lying there. Her feet were on the top step, head on the brick walkway. She stared heavenward with sightless eyes as if beseeching angels to save her. She looked as if she'd been mauled by a savage beast. Her shredded muslin drawers and chemise looked almost unrecognizable.

An auburn-haired woman stood in the doorway. She wore a dark green dress with pin tucks, velvet trim, and a wing collar. Annabelle Rouge, the "Lady in Red," was one of Louisville's most notorious madams. She stared at the dead girl as blood pooled under the body from numerous stab wounds. Young women huddled around her, some dressed only in their nightgowns, others in slips and petticoats.

Annabelle glared at the throng. Following her line of sight, I noticed the bicyclist. He trembled, face white. The bike lay on the ground, one wheel spinning uselessly.

Had he stumbled upon the body?

An officer drew the young man aside before I could reach him. I sidled as close as I could while remaining unobtrusive. The young man was employed by a messenger service. He'd been riding out to the Chute to deliver a message for Miss Annabelle when he discovered the body. Apparently satisfied, the officer let him go, then went around and interviewed the other bystanders. I admitted I had no idea who the victim was or who could've killed her.

Despite my deception, my skin prickled. The situation seemed too coincidental, like the murderer wanted someone to find the body.

How long had the corpse lain there? Not long, I surmised. But why Annabelle's house?

The crowd had dispersed, apparently bored with the machinations of police work. Only a few young men lingered, mainly to ogle Annabelle's nubile young charges.

There was no point questioning Annabelle tonight, given her vitriolic attacks on the officer and the unseen perpetrator. She gestured to the body, demanding to know when it would be removed. The officer looked flustered. Annabelle was one tough cookie when it came down to business. He was unable to deal with her overwhelming presence.

Back home, Stephen led me upstairs to the bedroom. I sat on the bed and he removed my shoes. Despite fatigue, thoughts raced through my brain. I tried to shove them aside, annoyed they wouldn't leave me alone.

Stephen sat next to me. He took my hand. "You look stressed."

I gave him a wry smile. "I feel stressed."

He brushed back my hair with his other hand, and kissed me. "Care to tell me about it?"

I closed my eyes, savoring this intimacy. "They found another body."

"Where?"

"Annabelle's bawdy house. On the front steps. This one was mauled, too."

"Wild dogs?"

I opened my eyes. "Dogs travel in packs. Someone would've noticed. No, ours is a lone wolf, or should I say shifter."

Stephen gave me a disapproving frown. "I doubt Sergeant Pierce will believe the Ripper or this murderer is a werewolf."

"You're probably right." I laid against the mattress and stared at the ceiling.

"It'd be easier if it were a pack of wild dogs." Stephen dimmed the gas light. "When would you like me to wake you?"

"This evening. Unless I get up earlier."

The sun had set when I awoke. The aroma of fried ham, beans, and freshly baked biscuits drifted upstairs, beckoning me downstairs to enjoy them.

I washed my hands and face at the washstand. Peering into the mirror, I rubbed the dark stubble on my chin. I hated shaving. Bloodletting was one thing. Cutting myself with a razor quite another.

After I managed to groom myself without injury, I went downstairs to eat. Questions nagged at me, interfering with my ability to enjoy the meal. The marks on this last victim matched the ones on the previous victim. This had to mean they'd both been killed by the same person.

Did the women know each other? Had they worked at the same brothel?

I'd no doubt the Ripper had murdered both women, most likely prostitutes, and was responsible for the missing Rosie.

"I suppose the murder will be in this evening's news," Stephen said.

He was right. The Cloak and Dagger was abuzz with conversation about the killing; politics and international wars were all but forgotten.

"You heard about it, too?" Francis asked. The murder had made headline news. This time a large photograph underneath the headline grabbed everyone's attention. It was one of Annabelle with an annoyed expression as she looked down at something unseen. The victim was not shown so as not to offend certain readers' delicate sensibilities. But the accompanying story was lurid enough, with mentions of "slayings too horrendous to mention in polite company." There were even contemptuous quotes by Annabelle, threatening the killer with legal action. Never mind she could be arrested for running a house of ill repute. Like other madams, Annabelle paid the police well to leave her alone.

The victim had been identified as twenty-four year old Madge Stevens, a lady of the night who worked around Grayson and Eighth Street.

"I think I'll pay Miss Annabelle a visit," I said. "I'll be back in a couple of hours."

"But it's time for me to go home," Francis protested.

"Keep track of your time. I'll pay you double." I hurried out the door before he could argue or agree.

Poor Francis. He'd every reason to be annoyed with me. I was supposed to be running a saloon, not playing detective. He was only in my employ.

But I couldn't stomach the thought of Jack the Ripper getting away with even one more murder.

I'd failed once before. I was determined that I wouldn't fail again.

Chapter Seven

Annabelle gave me a disapproving look when I told her I'd no interest in procuring one of her ladies, but wanted to discuss the recent murder.

We sat in her small office. She at her desk, papers and scented envelopes scattered on it while I sat on a nearby Grecian style sofa. A gilded bird cage stood in a corner, sans bird.

Annabelle brushed back a stray lock of hair. She regarded me with emerald green eyes, lashes thickened with mascara.

"I don't know why you bothered to come around." She fanned herself with an ostrich feather fan, despite the cool evening. "I've already told the police the girl didn't work for me. Anyone that wants to target me or my brothel will regret it to his dying day." She gave me a defiant look. "The other prostitutes may be scared, but not my girls. They know I watch out for them."

I reverted to my DI persona. "Yes, ma'am. But why do you think the killer left Madge's body on your steps?"

Annabelle waved a dismissive hand. "Someone must have a grudge against me. I wouldn't be surprised. My girls are the top of the line." She tried to sound nonchalant, but a tremor of fear tinged her voice.

"Any of your girls leave recently? Any disputes between you or the other madams?"

"No. For the most part, we get along." She laid her fan on the papers. "Not that business is doing so well lately. These murders have caused distrust between my ladies and our clients. How do we know one of them hasn't entertained the murderer and just been lucky? How do we know who we can trust?"

"Agreed." Not only could the murders cause dissension, they could also hurt the madams' and prostitutes' livelihoods as well as give the temperance unions even more power to demand their closure. "Did you ever hear of lass named Rosie, a girl from the tenements?" Again, I described Rachel's wayward daughter.

"Can't say that I have." Annabelle crossed her legs, giving me a peek at a slim ankle. "If she's one of us, she's probably using an alias. I'll ask my girls if they've seen or heard anything." She uncrossed her legs when she noticed I showed no interest in her physical charms. She shook head as if trying to fathom my lackluster response.

"Thank you." I pulled out my newspaper clipping and showed it to her. "Does she look familiar?"

Annabelle studied the picture, brow knitted in concentration. "Yes. She came in with this tall man." She stared at the ceiling, as if indicating his height. "Swarthy type, the kind who looked like he could hit a woman if she didn't obey him. I asked if he wanted a lady, and he laughed and asked if I wanted one." She shuddered. "That laugh, it was the most evil-sounding one I'd ever heard."

"He wanted you to buy the girl?"

Annabelle reached for her fan. "Now that you mention it, he didn't specifically say her. She seemed detached, as if we were sharing a secret joke she wanted no part of. When I said I didn't need another girl, they left."

"How long ago was this?"

She pursed her lips. "About a week and a half."

I stood, retrieving my fedora. "Thank you for your help. I'll be in touch."

Annabelle nodded, her expression indicating she was somewhere else, perhaps reliving that moment. I sensed a sadness in her, a weight pressing down on shoulders, which seemed to sag as she propped her elbows atop her desk and rested her chin on her hands, staring ahead, as if searching for answers in the jacquard wall covering.

I let myself out.

***

Francis swiped the rag across the bar with more ferocity than normal. From his narrowed eyes and frown, I guessed he wasn't happy.

"My feet hurt, and I'm tired," he complained. "Can I go home now?"

I nodded. "Did you write down your extra hours as I asked you to do?"

"Oh, yes." Removing his apron, he shot me another glare. "And I'll be sure to count my wages when you pay me."

"Get some rest and come in tomorrow afternoon." I'd ask Charlotte to open the tavern, or, if she were unavailable, would let it remained closed until later in the day. Francis deserved a reprieve. One of Stephen's retainers, he'd been the only servant allowed to join us when we left England, although Stephen never specified why.

Hours passed. I bustled about, serving alcohol, fixing sandwiches, bussing and wiping tables. It was only when I got a break, and a chance to grab a cup of coffee, I realized I hadn't seen Charlotte.

She was probably still angry with me for rebuffing her advances. I hadn't meant to hurt her feelings and promised to apologize when I saw her.

I couldn't help the one thought straying into my mind and shoved it aside. The bodies of my mysterious victim and Madge taunted me. The Ripper had to be responsible. But why dump the body on the steps of a bawdy house? Was he sending the madams and their girls a warning? Or was he taunting the police, growing bolder with each kill?

I paced the bar, towel slung over my left shoulder. Every time the door creaked open, my heart skipped a beat, and I hoped Charlotte would bounce in, her energy filling the room.

Each time, I was disappointed.

After closing the bar, I hurried to Big Edna's. A couple of prostitutes sat on the porch. They watched with suspicious eyes as I approached, but made no move to seduce me. Did they suspect something, or did they remember me from the night before?

"Have you seen Charlotte?" I asked.

They looked at each other and giggled. I waited, resisting the urge to go into detective inspector mode. Not that authority meant anything to them. I had none and they probably knew that as well.

"Changed your mind, did you?" One of the women sidled up to me, rubbing her body against mine. "I'm more fun than she is."

I'd no idea if she meant Charlotte or the woman sitting in the other rocker. I stepped away, and my seducer exhaled an exasperated sigh. "Is Big Edna available?"

"She's inside," the other prostitute said. "Go on in." She pointed to the entryway.

I thanked her and continued to the front door. A tasseled bell cord hung within reach and I pulled it.

A uniformed maid opened the door: I gave her my calling card. She ushered me into the receiving hall. After a few moments, the maid returned and led me to a parlor.

The room was filled with overstuffed sofas and wing chairs. A piano stood in one corner. Gaslight lamps flickered in sconces placed at intervals along the walls.

The door creaked open and Big Edna entered. Unlike her namesake, she was a petite woman, gray-haired and wrinkled. Her eyes were bright, posture ramrod straight.

"The maid said you wanted to see me, Mr. James." Her voice was strong. I sensed that same indomitable spirit I'd seen in Annabelle. She reached for a box of cigars, and offered me one. I politely declined.

"I'm sure you heard about my incident with Charlotte last night."

Edna returned the cigar box to its place. "Yes, but it seems to have worked itself out."

"She isn't angry?"

Edna looked surprised. "Why should she be?"

"I haven't seen her since last night," I said. "She usually comes around The Cloak and Dagger, but she didn't come in tonight."

"She's probably in her room. Wait here and I'll see."

After Edna had gone, I studied the Titian and Ruben paintings hanging on the walls, pictures of voluptuous women meant to stir men's carnal desires. They had the same effect on me as Annabelle's ankle – none.

When Edna returned a few moments later, her furrowed brow and pursed mouth warned me something was wrong. "She wasn't there. The maid hasn't seen her. None of the girls I've asked have seen her either."

My heart sank. If only I'd come earlier.

It was a foolish hope, but maybe she'd gone to my house. "May I use your phone?"

"Planning to call the police?" Big Edna gave me a suspicious look.

"A friend. He might know where she is."

"All right then, but I don't want any trouble."

"Me either, madam. There's been more than enough murders lately."

Stephen answered. "James residence."

"It's me," I said, line crackling with static. "Is Charlotte there?"

"No."

"I see." My heart plummeted into my stomach, sitting in my midsection like a heavy rock. "Thank you. I'll be home soon." I disconnected.

Edna must've seen the pained expression on my face. "Don't blame yourself, Mr. James. Charlotte can take care of herself." She tilted her head and studied me. "I get the impression you and Charlotte know each other. Am I right?"

"She was the first woman I met when I arrived in Louisville. Stood on the dock and asked me and my manservant if she could show us around." I smiled at the memory. "We declined, but I saw her again when I opened The Cloak and Dagger. She stopped by, and we've been acquaintances ever since." I hesitated to use the word "friends" because, to be honest, I'd no idea if Charlotte considered me one or not.

A knowing look came over Edna's face. "So you're the one she talks about, the former detective inspector." She sat on a divan, and folded her hands in her lap. "What brings you here to Louisville?"

"I was passing through and decided to stay."

"Or perhaps you were running from something." Edna gave me a penetrating look before breaking into a reassuring smile. "Don't look so nervous. Lots of people move for one reason or another. Many times it's to find themselves." She twisted an amethyst ring on her right ring finger. "You don't look like you've found yourself quite yet. I see it in your eyes, your face. You're a lost soul, still needing to search, but having no idea what for." She held up her hand. "Deny it all you want, but I see it in the faces of many men and young girls who come through those doors. For some, it's their first experience, and, when they leave, they're a bit wiser, worldlier. They don't realize it, but that simple act is a rite of passage."

"At this point, I'd rather find Charlotte and Rosie."

Edna quirked an eyebrow. "Rosie?"

For a second, I hoped she'd enlighten me. But when Edna didn't elaborate, I explained the situation, adding I'd promised Rosie's mother I'd try to find her. Like Annabelle and the others, Edna couldn't recall anyone by that name.

"You can ask my girls, but I doubt they'll know anything more than I do." Edna poured herself a glass of whiskey. "Are you a drinking man, Mr. James?"

"In moderation."

She handed me a glass. "I believe in hospitality."

"Thank you." I took a sip, savoring the mellow, smooth flavor.

"You're welcome. Might you be staying? Perhaps another girl might suit your fancy." Big Edna gave me an appraising look, as if gauging how much money I might part with today.

Of course, the hospitality came with conditions. I pulled out a wallet and extracted a roll of bills. I handed a few to her. "My apologies, but no thank you. Your ladies are quite lovely, but..." I faltered, fearing I'd said too much. Had the whiskey affected me? I could imagine Edna plying her customers with drink in an attempt to part them with their wages. As a bartender, I wasn't any different. We were all trying to make a living, and keep the temperance unions at bay.

Any displeasure Edna might've taken with my rejection of her offer was concealed by a thoughtful expression.

"I see," she said, tucking the money into a beaded purse. "That would certainly explain things." She gave me a wry smile. "I'm afraid I can't help you there, young man." She raised her hand again. "Now, now, don't worry. I won't tell. What does the Bible say about judging others? You've your preferences, and I respect that. You're more than welcome here any time."

"Thank you," I said, meaning every word. I'd probably need to return during my investigation. Knowing I was welcome made it easier.

She rang for the maid. "You find my Charlotte, you hear?" She grasped my hand between her dry, small ones. "She's a good girl. I want her back safe."

"I'll do my best." The maid escorted me to the door. I wondered how many more promises I'd make before they all collapsed under me.

***

"Charlotte's missing? Since when?" Stephen paused in his massage, hands resting on my shoulders. We sat in my bedroom. I was stripped to the waist, sitting cross-legged on the bed.

"I dropped her off at the brothel last night, but no one's seen her since." I tilted my head, stretching tense neck muscles. "She usually stops by The Cloak and Dagger every night."

"Perhaps she's busy." Stephen resumed his massage.

"She was angry with me for not taking her up on her offer." I ran my hand down my thigh and played with an imaginary loose thread on my trousers. "I had a talk with her madam, Big Edna tonight."

"You didn't tell her about us." Stephen's voice was sharp, fingernails digging into my skin.

"Ow!" I winced and then glared at him. "Of course not. But she guessed."

Stephen jerked his hands back, face dark. "What if she starts gossiping? It could get around, get back to people like Sergeant Pierce. What then? He'll arrest us."

"He can't, not if we're not buggering each other in public," I argued. "And we're always discreet."

Stephen's harsh laugh sliced my soul. "He'd lie. His word against ours. Who do you think they'd believe?" He stood and faced me. "I can't lose you." Bitterness filled his voice, and he seemed much older than he appeared, as if the responsibility of being a master vampire had taken its toll. "Once a master vampire turns someone, they're bonded for life. If you die, so will I. The same thing will happen to you if I die. People kill vampires."

I fought back rising nausea. Despite her promise, could I trust Big Edna?

"We can't keep our lives secret forever," I argued. "Sooner or later, people will find out about us."

This apparently triggered Stephen's fight response. He grabbed my shoulders and shook me. "We can and we will." His fangs dropped, and he glowered at me with such malevolence, I averted my face, sickened by his rage. "Otherwise I'll kill you myself."

I sat, disbelieving, awash in dread. He really meant to hurt me. Licking dry lips, I struggled to find my voice. "Please go." My words rasped in my throat, painful not only physically, but psychologically. I pushed away the only man I'd ever cared about. But I couldn't deal with this sudden change, his threat icing my spine. Perhaps he'd said it out of fear, but that didn't make the warning any less palatable.

Stephen balked. "I'm sorry. I didn't mean to upset you." He sat next to me.

I waved my hand, not wanting to hear any apology. The bedsprings creaked as Stephen got up, but made no move to leave.

Several agonizing moments passed. I stared at a fissure in the plaster, but couldn't bring myself to look at him.

"You'd understand my position better if you'd seen your family executed for being different." The door clicked as he shut it behind him.

I lay back against the mattress. Stephen had never talked about his family. Perhaps the memories were too painful. I thought of Grace, and tears filled my eyes. Sighing, I reached for my undershirt and pulled it on. Wiping my eyes with the back of my hand, I shoved the haunting memory into the recesses of my mind.

Everything had to be all right. Jack the Ripper would be stopped, Charlotte and Rosie would be found, and I'd settle back into my routine life as a saloon owner.

Too bad I couldn't believe that.

Chapter Eight

A few hours later, Big Edna called to tell me one of her girls had encountered a body on the steps of her brothel. The discovery must've been recent judging by all the hysterical crying in the background. When I arrived at the brothel, I felt emotionally battered, memories of Grace and Stephen's outburst, along with lack of sleep taking their toll.

Edna sat in a rocker on the porch. Her gnarled hands gripped the arm rails. Despite her straight posture and resolute expression, she looked small and vulnerable. The girls gathered behind her, peering with wide, frightened eyes at the disemboweled corpse sprawled on the steps. The woman's face had been clawed, ribbons of flesh hanging loose, throat slashed.

I ran up the walk to the verandah. "You might want to take the girls inside. Have you called the police?"

Instead of answering me, Edna stood and clapped her hands. "Inside, ladies." She shooed them indoors, and pulled the door shut behind them.

I knelt beside the body. Like Madge, this one, too, wore only a chemise and drawers. I couldn't surmise whether she'd been murdered before or after sex, or dressed this way for reasons currently known to only the killer. I just didn't know. "One of yours?"

Edna shook her head. "I've never seen her before." She crossed herself. "And so soon after poor Madge."

A chill ran up my spine. Was it possible this was one of Annabelle's ladies? Could the murderer be hoping to create dissension between the two brothels?

I joined Edna on the porch after a cursory examination of the body. We sat on a wicker rocker. On a more pleasant night, we might enjoy mint juleps.

"I apologize for not offering you any refreshments," Edna said, as if reading my mind.

"Given the circumstances we are in it is quite all right."

Edna rubbed her hands, a worried look on her face. "I wonder if this is one of Annabelle's girls."

"I don't know," I admitted. "But since Madge was found on her steps, it seems likely this victim is one of hers."

The madam shuddered. "Who would do such a thing? These poor girls are just trying to make a living like everybody else."

Our conversation was interrupted by the clatter of horses' hooves and rattle of carriage wheels nearing the brothel. Police whistles punctured the silence.

Sergeant Pierce jumped off the wagon and ran up the walk. He glanced at the body, and his face paled. "Good Lord!" Seeing Edna, he touched the brim of his patrol cap. "Excuse my language, ma'am." I looked over his shoulder to see Annabelle approaching. Her eyes widened upon seeing the body. She clasped a ringed hand over her mouth.

"Livvie!"

Sergeant Pierce turned to her. "Do you know her?"

Annabelle glared at him. "Of course I do! She's Olivia Hendricks. Livvie, for short. She was working tonight." She pointed an accusing finger at Edna. "Don't tell me this is retaliation for what happened to Madge."

Edna stiffened. "You know me better than that."

Sergeant Pierce stepped between them. "That's enough." He placed his hand beneath Edna's elbow, and steered her toward the house. "Come inside, and I'll take your statement." He looked over his shoulder at us. "Wait there."

Pulling out a notebook and pencil, a police officer approached Annabelle. She nodded her head in response to his questions, body contracting when something seemed to upset her.

The officer approached me after interviewing her. He flipped his notebook open to a new page.

"Your name and address, sir."

I gave him the information. He arched an eyebrow at the mention of St. James Court, but continued.

"Do you know the victim?" He glanced at the body, now covered by a white sheet, and shuddered. Perhaps this was his first murder. The shock wouldn't manifest itself until later, when he'd find himself vomiting, trying to purge the horrible memory from his mind and nightmares. It'd happened to me, not only the time I ran across my first murder victim, but also at the sight of Mary Kelly. Anyone who could look upon the eviscerated and mangled remains without feeling sick or horrified lacked any human conscience. Even as a vampire, I couldn't help but pity the Ripper's victims. True, Grace's murder compelled me to stop him, but I also pursued the Ripper for the other casualties he left behind in dark, dank alleys.

"No. I only learned her name when Annabelle arrived."

The officer gave me an askance glance. "May I ask what you were doing here tonight?"

He assumed I came here for one of the ladies. "Edna asked me to come. I'm trying to help her learn who murdered Madge."

"That's a police matter." He shut his notebook. The officer gave me an aggrieved look, as if my mere presence contaminated the murder scene. A memory seemed to niggle his mind. "Aren't you the owner of The Cloak and Dagger?"

"Yes."

The officer rubbed his chin, pencil tip angled downward. "Sergeant Pierce talks about you. Says you used to work for Scotland Yard before you came here."

"I hope he says only good things," I joked.

"He does, sir. Just funny finding you at a crime scene when that's not your job anymore, if you'll forgive my bluntness."

I gave what I hoped my most ingratiating smile. "Must be that detective instinct."

The officer didn't look impressed, and went to find and question more witnesses. I walked over to Annabelle to see how she was doing.

Annabelle hugged herself and rocked back and forth. "What kind of animal would do this?"

She meant what kind of a human animal, but she was far more intuitive than she realized. These were similar to the marks I'd seen in Whitechapel. Only this time, they were more brutal, as if the creature were consumed by fury.

"One we plan to catch," I promised.

She gave me an incredulous look. "You? You're not a police officer. How can you help?"

"I used to be with Scotland Yard. I had a similar case."

She arched an eyebrow. "Then I'll trust you and Sergeant Pierce to find the killer so my girls can start working again. I've restricted them to the house as it is. They are not happy about it, even though they know it is for their protection."

"Good idea."

By now a small crowd had gathered. The curious, the macabre seekers – onlookers craning to get a view of the body, except there was nothing to see, at least nothing lurid. Big Edna didn't want a spectacle like there'd been at Annabelle's. She had her reputation to protect, although, to be fair, so did Annabelle. A mauled corpse on one's doorstep could damage an already tenuous relationship between the madams and police, including the local citizenry.

Sergeant Pierce emerged from the house. The officer whispered something to him. He nodded and announced we were free to go.

Annabelle and I passed the slack faces and dull eyes of the milling throng. Relief flooded her face once we were alone, our shadows leading us.

"Like vultures. Circling and waiting." Her voice dripped with disgust.

"Death draws the curious," I admitted. "You become used to it."

She gave me a disgusted look. "Why do humans find death, especially violent death, so interesting?"

"Perhaps it's because of their own mortality."

She fell silent. After seeing her home, I continued on to St. James Court. Annabelle believed Edna responsible for Livvie's death for one reason or another. But what motivation could Edna have? She didn't seem like an "eye for an eye" type.

Stephen had tea ready when I arrived home. I needed something to warm me after seeing that gruesome death scene.

"Do you think Annabelle and Edna will keep their girls off the street?" Stephen asked when I told him about this latest murder.

I took a sip of my Earl Grey. "Most likely with these recent murders. At least for a few nights."

He handed me a tray of tea biscuits. "Wonder why he's dumping the bodies at the brothels. Is he trying to send a message?

I reached for a biscuit. I ended my work day in a similar way. Perhaps it was an ingrained habit.

Seeing I wasn't answering his question, Stephen continued hypothesizing. "The Ripper does seem to be changing his modus operandi." He reached for his cup. "Maybe he decided the old way didn't work. It's been ten years. He's had time to improve his technique."

"Which means he'll be even more difficult to stop."

Stephen lifted his cup in my direction. "You can't blame yourself. You were bound to the rules and regulations of the force, just like Sergeant Pierce. Although I'd doubt he'd become a vampire to catch a murderer."

I stiffened. "You know perfectly well why I came to you."

Stephen smiled. "Of course. It's because you were attracted to me."

***

The next morning, the incessant rattling of the door knocker jerked me out of a restless sleep. I rolled over, muttering, and tried to go back to sleep.

A knock on the door made me debate throwing my slipper at the wood frame. "Sergeant Pierce is waiting for you," Stephen said from the other side.

"Coming!" I sat up and reached for my slippers. My robe hung on a hook behind the door. I slipped it on as I descended the stairs.

Sergeant Pierce waited in the living room. He didn't wear his uniform. Was this a social call?

"Would you like some tea or coffee?" I asked.

"No, thank you." He sat in the wing chair next to the chesterfield. "I wanted to let you know we're looking for your young lady friend, Charlotte. Big Edna reported her missing."

"Missing?" My stomach lurched. What if she'd become the Ripper's next victim?

He gave me a sympathetic look, then looked away while twisting his derby in his hands. He didn't want his face to give away what I already knew he thought. "We're hoping she's safe, but what with these murders..."

"Have you identified the first victim?"

"Not yet. We suspect she was also a prostitute, given they seem to be the only victims." He gave a short laugh. "Almost like your Ripper. But he wouldn't be here in Kentucky."

I remained silent, hoping my expression didn't give away my true thoughts. If Sergeant Pierce didn't think the Ripper committed these crimes, I'd need more than theories to convince him. "Any leads?"

The Sergeant shrugged. "I'm afraid not. From the injuries, we assume it's probably some kind of animal. A wild dog, perhaps. Maybe the killer is using a canine as a weapon. We'll put it and this city out of its misery once we find it. Our problem should be solved."

A wild animal, yes. But not the kind he was thinking of. Ordinary bullets wouldn't destroy this one.

"But why attack only prostitutes?"

"The only reason I can think of is because they're alone, vulnerable and it's late at night. These dogs sense fear, see them as easy prey." He spoke with authority, as if he'd seen such dogs in action.

"It seems feasible." It was a logical theory. I might have believed him if I didn't have any other evidence.

Sergeant Pierce stood. "Guess I'd better be getting home. Night shift tonight."

I saw him to the door.

"What did he want?" Stephen asked as he descended the stairs.

"Charlotte's missing. Apparently, Edna told him. I guess losing one girl convinced her it might be a good idea to tell the police."

Stephen came up behind me, placing his large, strong hands on my shoulders. "Worried about her?"

I covered his hand in mine. "Of course. I'll have to tell Francis. You know how he feels about her."

Stephen's arms moved down to encircle my waist, and he drew me closer. He nipped at my neck. "Why concern yourself with humans? You're no longer one of them."

I leaned my head back, hair falling against his chest. "Can't help it. Don't forget, I was one of them."

"Of course." He smiled at me, our differences in height obvious.

Stephen ran a finger down my temple. He turned me to face him. "Perhaps this will take your mind off of them." He cupped my face and kissed me – a slow, deep, passionate kiss. All my worries, anger, and frustration melted into that kiss, into the heat of his mouth.

His lips moved down my chin, to my throat, then my neck, the place he liked to bite, careful to never leave a mark. A pinch of pain soon gave way to pleasure as he drew blood.

I ran my hands up his back, skin warm against my palms.

He offered his hand, palm turned upward. I traced thick blue veins on his wrist, pulse throbbing beneath my touch. My fangs dropped, and that familiar need coursed through my body, fueled by adrenaline. Taking the offered hand, I punctured the vein, blood spraying into my mouth.

Stephen shuddered, fangs still piercing my neck. I gripped him tighter with my other hand, my mind heady with the intoxicating scent of blood.

After a few moments, Stephen pulled away. I looked at him. Blood trickled from the corners of his mouth. I stopped drinking and wiped the blood from his mouth with my finger.

"Still hungry?" he asked, his grin mischievous.

I licked my finger and gave him a seductive smile. "Are you glad you're with me?"

"It was your decision," he said. He placed his finger upon my lips. "And for that, I'm glad."

"So am I." I leaned against him, breathing in the smell of soap and salt. Detective Sergeant Albertson had rescued me from a life of crime. Stephen had saved me from a life of self-inflicted guilt and despair.

He cupped the back of my head, fingers running through my hair. The cotton of his shirt pressed against my cheek. After a moment, I looked at him, our eyes meeting. He smiled before leaning down to kiss me again.

"You know I'll always look after you," he said.

I nodded. "And you know I'd do the same."

I'd defend my friends to the death.

Chapter Nine

Francis seemed in a better mood than he had been in the previous night. He pushed a mug of coffee and the *Courier-Journal* toward me.

"Any new information?" Scanning the front page, I tied my apron. This time, the murder had warranted more column space and a larger headline. According to the police, the attacks were being blamed on a pack of wild dogs. No mention of Jack the Ripper.

I looked at him. "Wild dogs? What nonsense."

He nodded. "But quite feasible. And it will keep people from panicking."

Francis had a point. The last thing anyone wanted was a mob fueled by hysteria and terror; unable to think logically. Not that most people cared about what happened to prostitutes. But if they could find a way to blame the madams for the deaths...

"Have you heard from Charlotte?" Francis asked.

I couldn't tell him Sergeant Pierce's bad news. "Not yet." I took a sip of coffee and grimaced. Francis made it strong. I'd suggested he market it as a cure for hangovers.

"That's a bad sign." Francis pulled on his coat. The temperature was supposed to drop tonight, a warning of the impending winter. He donned his homburg. "I'll be off then, Mr. James. See you tomorrow."

"Good night." I looked around the bar. Tonight seemed like it'd be quiet. I reread the story of Olivia's murder and how the police compared it to Madge's. They currently had no suspects. The reporter closed the article with a warning to young ladies not to venture out alone at night, lest they fall victim to feral dogs or the sordid life that had precipitated the killings.

The door creaked open, and Sergeant Pierce entered. He wore his uniform, and the patrons gave him suspicious looks, but he ignored them.

He removed his hat and stared at the floor, scraping the sole of his shoe against the wood. Not wanting to say it but knowing he had to do it. "I've some bad news, Mr. James."

A stone plummeted into my stomach, splashing acid. I leaned over the bar counter, palms flat on the newspaper, obscuring Olivia's smiling face. "Charlotte's dead."

Sergeant Pierce looked taken aback. He twisted his cap as he looked at me, his expression glum. "No, sir. I'm afraid she's been arrested for murder."

The newspaper nearly skidded to the floor as I pushed myself to a standing position. "Murder? What on earth makes you think our dear Charlotte is capable of murder?"

"I'm sorry. I know how much you like her. But we found her with a crucial piece of evidence."

I stared at him, incredulous. "Have you told Edna?" My mind rebelled against the idea Charlotte would kill anyone. But then my detective persona reminded me one had to suspect everyone, even friends.

Sergeant Pierce nodded. "I don't like it, either. It was the perfect crime to get rid of any competition if she really is the killer."

"Don't forget Rosie," I reminded him. "We don't know if she's a prostitute. And why would Charlotte kill one of Edna's ladies? That doesn't make sense."

He gave me an exasperated look. "Yes, well, there are flaws in our theory. But you know how investigations are, especially with no or few leads. We need to work with what we have."

"What about our mysterious stranger?" I tapped the newspaper. "Or these dogs mentioned in the article."

"Are you going to tell the newspapers?"

"No. For now, I think we'll focus on the feral dog angle."

I folded the newspaper and tucked it on a shelf under the bar. No one, not even the Sergeant, could convince me Charlotte killed those women. No, that mysterious man, whom I still believed to be the Ripper, was probably responsible for the murders and Rosie's disappearance. Only problem was I couldn't prove it.

"I assume you'll want to visit her," Sergeant Pierce said. "Normal visiting hours, of course." He touched the brim of his patrol cap. "Good night, sir. Sorry about the bad news."

I hardly heard the door open and shut. The rest of the shift I moved around in a daze, filling orders, but unaware of what I was doing. That I didn't accidentally give a customer who ordered beer a whiskey was a miracle.

The other problem was I couldn't risk walking about in daylight. It was only a matter of time before the cloudy skies cleared. Perhaps Francis could go for me. I'd give him a call later. Not that I wanted to give him the bad news about Charlotte. But one of us had to see her, and I suspected she'd be more receptive at seeing him than me.

I closed the Cloak and Dagger early, shooing out the few customers on the pretense of not feeling well. It wasn't a lie. My insides felt as if they'd been lacerated, then twisted until the pain became almost unbearable. Charlotte sat in jail, accused of a crime I knew she hadn't committed. Never mind what my detective side argued. My human side refused to believe Charlotte guilty.

She would most likely hang if they found her guilty.

Walking home, I tried to think of how to draw out the Ripper. Bait him? No, he probably wouldn't fall for that. The Ripper's intelligence made him a dangerous adversary unlike most criminals. I had to find another way.

If only I could find Rosie or learn the name of the first victim. I might make an important connection if I was able to do that. But aside from the Ripper possibly arriving via steamboat and Rosie's disappearance, along with the prostitute connection, I had little to work with to solve this crime.

When I worked for Scotland Yard, I'd access to police information. Here, I'd no jurisdiction. Sergeant Pierce shared what information he could, but no more. Doing so might impede the investigation.

I was halfway home when I decided to go to Edna's and Annabelle's brothels. I wanted to look at the murdered women's rooms to search for any clues.

Annabelle's bawdy house was closer. She greeted me at the door, dark circles under her eyes. Most likely the police had questioned her extensively, not only about Livvie's murder but also Madge's.

"I hope you haven't brought any bad news," she said, ushering me into her office.

"Not likely," I assured her. "With your permission, I'd like to take a look at Olivia's room."

Annabelle nodded, expression weary. Her hands shook as she pulled a ring of keys off a hook. She gestured for me to follow.

Olivia's room was on the second floor at the end of a long hallway. Annabelle fitted the key in the lock. I couldn't help but feel a sense of foreboding, that we'd open the door and find Olivia dead, sprawled across her bed.

But the room was empty, although the eerie feeling remained, compounded by the lingering scent of powder and perfume hanging in the air.

The room was done in burgundy and gold. The bed taking the most space with its large, golden rails, and decorated with small lace-trimmed throw pillows.

A small closet revealed a few dresses, boas, and hats. The dresser was filled with petticoats and shifts. I didn't bother looking through those. Instead, I turned my attention to the small writing desk.

Annabelle stood in the doorway, looking unsure whether to leave or stay.

"I won't steal anything," I assured her. "If you want to go back, please feel free."

She crossed her arms over her chest. "I don't like the idea of a man being here alone, unescorted."

I smiled at the irony. In proper society, she and her girls would be the ones needing escorts. But here, in her world, the situation was reversed.

"Then stay."

She looked down the hall, then back at me. "All right, Mr. James. I'll leave you to it. Close the door when you're finished and let me know when you are finished so I can lock the door again."

I nodded and she left. Though not before giving me a final warning look. I had to admit to a certain feeling of satisfaction she trusted me, especially given how vulnerable she and the other ladies of the night were.

Feeling around in the desk drawer, my fingers touched a small book wedged in the back. I pulled out a diary with a purple floral cover and lavender paper. The pages were filled with flowing feminine cursive writing.

I sat on the bed, springs creaking beneath me. Glancing through the diary, I read glimpses into Olivia's life. She'd moved to Louisville from a small town in central Kentucky, hoping to make a name for herself as a singer. Why she hadn't gone to Lexington, which was closer? Louisville had a number of dance halls and I assumed many girls tried their luck there before finding themselves forced to seek employment elsewhere.

She seemed like a nice young lady, one who'd dreamed of going to Paris, marrying and having children. She'd never have the chance of doing any of that now.

If I expected to learn any sordid details of her life, the diary revealed nothing. Those encounters she kept in the privacy of her mind.

I closed the journal, and replaced it in the writing desk. Next, I pulled out a small lacquered box filled with jewelry. Something didn't feel right. Hefting the case in my hand, I rapped on the bottom of the box. The hollow sound made me suspect a false bottom, and, after poking and prodding, I opened a secret compartment.

A piece of paper fluttered to the floor, and I bent to pick it up. Turning it over, my heart froze.

It was a tintype of Livvie with two other girls. One was the still unknown murder victim and the other someone who might possibly fit the description of Rosie.

Olivia knew Rosie? Did that mean Rosie worked for Annabelle at one time? But what about Madge?

I tucked the picture into my coat pocket and debated taking the diary. I'd promised Annabelle I wouldn't steal anything, but I meant anything of value.

My conscience and I didn't war for very long. The diary joined the ferrotype. Satisfied I'd seen what I needed, I stepped into the hallway, and pulled the door shut.

If Annabelle cared I'd stolen anything, she remained quiet. She'd probably throw away Livvie's belongings or give them to charity, keeping any valuables for herself.

Madge's room was similar to Livvie's, except Madge didn't keep a diary. She did have an address book, filled with names. Clients or relatives, who knows? Edna had told me she didn't think Madge had any friends. She kept to herself.

What had drawn Madge to this wayward life? What circumstances had changed so she'd give up whatever dream she had to service men and possibly women?

I'd hope to find some photograph possibly connecting the two women. Unlike Olivia, Madge was an intensely private person.

"Find everything you needed?" Edna asked when I returned.

"For the most part." An idea occurred to me and I pulled out the tintype. I showed it to her. "Do you recognize any of them?"

Edna studied the photograph, her lips pursed in concentration. After a moment, she pointed to the girl with dark hair fashioned in the Gibson Girl style.

"That's Rosie."

My heart did a double beat. "Are you sure?"

She gave me an annoyed look. "I'm old, Mr. James, but not so far gone I can't remember names. Remember, I have seven young ladies to keep track of. And if I could keep track of ten children, then seven is nothing."

"Was Rosie one of your girls?"

Edna shook her head. "Oh, no. But she would talk about her sister. No, half-sister, I think it was." She pointed to the other girl, the first murder victim. "That's her." She leaned back in her chair. "Name escapes me... I remember now. Her name was Amelia!"

My heart nearly stopped, and I pressed a hand to my chest, as if encouraging it to keep pumping. Adrenaline coursed through me. "Sisters?"

"Same father but different mothers. Rosie used to talk about how wonderful her and Amelia's father was, even though she'd never met him. Said he was British." She shrugged. "Young ladies will say anything to impress their friends."

Knees weak, I grabbed the back of a chair. Serendipity, like luck, was capricious. "Have you seen Rosie's father?"

Edna shook her head. "Just her stepfather. She called him a drunk, said he wasn't worth nothing. Drowned in the Ohio River a few years ago, I believe."

I tried to recall any death by drowning, but couldn't. Most likely Rosie's stepfather had abandoned the family, and she'd made up the tale to compensate for feelings of anger and fear of abandonment. Her story about a British father could also be that, too.

"The only reason I know about her supposed real father is I heard her telling some john he was British and from London." Edna shook her head. "That was when she was working for me. It was on a trial basis. Truth is, I didn't think she was suitable for such a life."

I must've looked surprised. "Not every girl is suited for this kind of work, Mr. James. It can put an incredible amount of strain on mind and body. Rosie tried to act tough, but she was too delicate, too much of a dreamer, despite her growing up in the tenement."

I asked if she'd be willing to tell Sergeant Pierce about Amelia, but she declined.

"It'd be better if you told him, but don't reveal your sources. I hope you find Rosie. Most likely the poor girl doesn't know what to do with herself."

Or maybe she does. Perhaps Rosie wasn't as innocent as she seemed, if Rachel's description was any indication.

I poured myself a glass of rye whiskey as soon as I got home and settled on the couch with Livvie's diary.

Stephen glanced at my reading material. "I thought you were more Doyle or Wells."

I gave him a stern look over the top of Livvie's journal. "Amusing." Lowering the book, I patted the cushion next to me.

Stephen sat and listened as I told him about Charlotte and the supposed identity of the murdered girl and her relationship to the missing Rosie. I showed him the photograph.

"Are you going to talk to the photographer?" he asked.

"Someone also has to visit Charlotte in jail," I pointed out. While I still voted Francis go, I needed someone to run the bar. And Stephen would be the last person I'd put behind the counter at The Cloak and Dagger.

"I wonder who paid for the pictures." Stephen took the tintype and studied it closely, as if he could read the girls' thoughts.

I went to the bar, and pour us each a drink. "Whoever it is," I said, "maybe I'll find out when I go to the studio."

"Are you going to tell Sergeant Pierce?" Stephen took the whiskey I handed him.

"Yes, after I talk to Charlotte and the studio photographer." I sat and picked up Olivia's private book.

Stephen sipped his drink and watched as I read accounts of a young woman I'd never meet. Back at the bawdy house, I'd only given her diary a cursory glance, skipping pages and scanning chunks of text. I started from the beginning.

Olivia had arrived in Louisville three months ago. Supposedly, she'd had an audition with an impresario but instead found herself the victim of unwanted sexual advances. She'd been unable to return home since she'd spent all her money to come to Louisville. While wandering the streets, looking for a place to sleep, she ran across a young woman who took her to Annabelle's. She liked the older woman and decided to stay, first earning her keep by light housekeeping and cooking, then moving on to servicing clients.

I turned the book over on my lap, and stared at the ceiling. How does a girl go from being a well-bred Christian to being willing to sell her body? Olivia had mentioned not wanting her parents to worry about her, which meant she never corresponded with them. Most likely, she didn't want them finding out about her new life and shaming the family. Grace had been the same, only writing me when she realized she'd no choice.

Had Olivia's parents searched for her? If only I knew her last name, I could ask Sergeant Pierce.

I resumed reading the diary, hoping to learn how she met Amelia and Rosie. But the only mention of them was a picnic they planned before one of them returned to England. This entry was dated two weeks ago, and, except for one in which she talked about a dream of living in Paris, was the final entry in the diary.

If there were a heaven, I hoped Olivia was in the City of Lights.

The whiskey lulled me to sleep. I put my glass on the table. After wishing Stephen good night, and wondering if he ever slept, I trudged upstairs. After putting the diary atop my bureau, and undressing, I climbed into bed.

Within minutes, I was asleep, dreaming of young girls giggling and posing before the camera.

Ladies who believed they had an eternity before them.

Chapter Ten

I awoke shortly after noon. Stephen had made chicken soup and sandwiches made with thick slabs of bread spread with butter and cheese. We ate in silence.

Stephen spoke first. "Maybe you should let Sergeant Pierce talk to the photography studio."

"People tend to be suspicious of the police. I might have better luck."

"Why do you care about these people?" Stephen began clearing the table. "Even if you stop the Ripper, it won't bring Grace back."

"What if I were murdered? Wouldn't you want to know the truth?" Stephen's lack of emotion failed to surprise me after all these years. Until I'd come into his life, Stephen had lived alone, detached not only from humans, but from other vampires as well. He told me he had a staff of servants, but they never dealt with him face to face, given his preternatural status. Indeed, the only servant he interacted with was Francis. Stephen had encouraged me to hire Francis as a bartender, despite the young man having almost no experience. In a way, I felt sorry for Stephen. Various people had acted as my surrogate family: Detective Sergeant Albertson, my former co-workers at Scotland Yard, Francis, Stephen, and even Charlotte. They could never replace my family, but they helped me forget the pain of losing one.

How many years had Stephen suffered in silence?

Lunch finished, I went into the living room. Stephen joined me a few minutes later, carrying a tray laden with an electroplated coffeepot, a creamer, sugar bowl, and two cups.

Coffee served, Stephen sat in the armchair. He crossed his legs, and rested his hands on the upholstered arms. Eyes closed, he seemed deep in thought.

I mentally prepared myself to go out. Stephen was right. I'd no obligation to solve the murders or to find Rosie. But if I didn't, guilt would gnaw at my conscience and I'd become unbearable to live with.

Stephen had a choice. He could live with my idiosyncrasies for a short while, or he could live with a miserable, guilt-ridden vampire for eternity.

I finished my coffee. "If Francis calls, tell him I'm running some errands. If Sergeant Pierce stops by, tell him I'm indisposed."

Stephen merely nodded as I shrugged into my outer wear. I put the tintype in my coat pocket. He opened his eyes when I blew a gentle breath across his forehead, causing bangs to stir. Giving him a wry grin, I bent down, and gave him a quick kiss.

"Be careful," he said, lips dry against mine.

"Always."

A few minutes later I caught a mule car and headed toward downtown Louisville.

Davidson Photography Studios had positioned itself in a strategic location not far from the wharf. A cameraman directed two young ladies to move closer together in front of the steamboat they must've arrived on. Had he taken the photograph of Olivia, Amelia, and Rosie?

I headed across the street. Davidson Photography Studio was housed in a long one-story building, with gilded lettering across the plate glass window, and a green awning to keep out the sun.

I opened the door to the studio. A bell tinkled merrily. A faint odor, as of rotten eggs, assailed my sensitive nose, but I ignored it.

The interior was divided into a reception area and photography studio, a thick black curtain separating the two. At the sound of my entrance, a plump young woman emerged from behind the partition. She pushed back a lock of hair and smiled. I nodded and removed my hat.

"Hello."

"Help you, mister?" She gave me an appraising glance. "Come to get your picture taken?" She planted her hands on her hips and gave an approving nod. "You're quite handsome, would make a perfect model."

"Thank you, but no. I'm wondering if you could help me."

She frowned, the look of someone who's possibly lost a sale and isn't happy. "I'll try."

I pulled out the ferrotype, and showed it to her. "Do you recognize them?"

The young woman studied the tintype. She handed the picture to me. "They were here. Came with a man."

"Do you remember anything about the session? Who paid for it?"

"I remember I didn't like him." She shuddered, making a face. "He scared me."

My fingers tightened on the tintype. "Tall, menacing?"

She looked at me, eyes wide. "How'd you know? Spoke in an accent almost like yours. Only thicker."

"How did the girls act around him?" I put the ferrotype on the counter.

The shop girl pointed to Amelia. "She seemed really close to him. Hung onto his arm, called him 'Father.' You could see the admiration on her face." She turned her attention to Rosie. "She seemed hurt somehow, watching them. Jealous, I'd say."

"What about the third girl? How did she act?"

The young woman tapped her finger on the counter and frowned. "Quiet. I got the sense she felt grateful for being there, as if they were doing her a favor."

"How many prints were made?" I assumed three, one for each of them.

She nodded at the tintype. "Just that one." She gave me another suspicious look. "How'd you come across it?"

"It was given to me," I lied. "Thank you. You've been quite helpful."

It was only after I was a block away, I realized I'd forgotten to set up a photography session.

***

My visit to the photography studio concluded, I headed to the police station and jail. Luckily, the weather remained bleak and cloudy. But I couldn't trust to luck.

The jailer seemed uninterested in my reason for being there. After signing in, he told me to wait in the visiting room. He returned with a shackled Charlotte. After warning us we only had five minutes, he exited, locking the door behind him.

Despite looking tired, Charlotte seemed glad to see me. I noticed she'd lost weight and her face had an unhealthy pallor.

She sat at the table across from me. Her handcuffs clanked as she set her wrists on the table. I noticed a burly guard watching us, one hand on his truncheon in case we tried anything foolish.

Strands of brittle hair fell over her eyes and she brushed them back with her forearm. "Nice to see you again, Nathan." She attempted a smile, but it came out as more of a grimace.

"I'm sorry." I wanted to reach out, touch her hand, give her comfort, but the rules stated we couldn't touch each other, not being related by blood or marriage.

"I suppose you know why I'm here?"

"Sergeant Pierce said you were found with a bloody knife."

She gave a snort, garnering a glare from her guard. "So I was. But someone drugged me, and placed the knife in my hand. When I came to, the police surrounded me. I tried to tell them I'd no idea where the knife came from, but they didn't believe me." She gave me a beseeching look. "You know I'm innocent. Can't you persuade Sergeant Pierce?"

The conviction in her voice convinced me she was telling the truth. This meant someone had probably set her up.

"I promise I'll do what I can."

Charlotte gave a sad smile as she looked past me to the door that could lead to her freedom. "Don't make promises you can't keep."

The guard approached. "Five minutes." He gestured for Charlotte to stand. She obeyed. I watched him lead her out another door that led to her cell.

Charlotte glanced over her shoulder, and I lifted my right hand in farewell. A meaningless gesture, perhaps, but also a vow to keep my promise.

***

Sergeant Pierce didn't look happy I'd kept information from him. He acquiesced when I assured him I'd only discovered this news recently.

"It's a difficult enough investigation," he said, "without people withholding possible evidence." He gave me a hard look. "Believe me, Mr. James, I appreciate your help, but that doesn't mean you can start your own investigation, and which can possibly interfere with ours."

I bristled slightly. "I've no intention of interfering with your investigation."

He sighed, running a hand through his hair. "No, of course not." He dropped his arm on the desk, scattering a sheaf of papers.

"But you wouldn't believe the number of calls we've received from people claiming to have seen those wild dogs mentioned in the paper." He tapped a rolled-up edition of the *Courier-Journal.* "There are even editorials praising the death of those prostitutes and the hope more will die." Sergeant Pierce turned weary eyes to me. "Do you know how hard it is to do your job when there are people who don't care?"

"I care." Maybe it would cost me my life, but I wanted to see justice for these young women.

"You may be the only one. Aside from the madams and the other girls, of course."

"What do you think of Rosie disappearing around the same time as Amelia's murder?"

Sergeant Pierce pulled out a pipe. He packed a wad of tobacco into the bowl, movements methodical. "It's suspicious." He struck a wood match, lighting the pipe. "That could give us a motive."

"They were half sisters. From what the lady at the photography studio says, Rosie seemed jealous of Amelia."

"Jealous enough to murder?" Sergeant Pierce released a plume of bluish smoke in the air.

"It's possible. And did she have help from her father, who may be our mysterious man?"

"Can't say for sure he was involved." But the sergeant didn't look convinced.

"Still think it's wild dogs?"

He took another drag on his pipe. "Of course not. But do you want us scaring the masses with talk of, say, Jack the Ripper?" He gave me a knowing look. "The last thing we need is for people to panic."

"That may not be a problem as long as our killer refrains from murdering anyone of a higher social class."

"We're hoping to make an arrest before it reaches that point." The sergeant tapped ashes into a glass ashtray, grayish-white flecks scattering across his desk.

"When do you plan to release Charlotte? You know she's innocent."

Sergeant Pierce drew a visible breath. He was probably counting to ten, trying to calm nerves I'd ruffled. "Your lady friend was found with a bloody knife most likely used in the killings."

"She said someone drugged her, and put the knife in her hands."

"Told us the same story."

I decided to try another tactic. "Don't you think if she really was the killer she would try to get rid of the weapon instead of being found with it?"

Sergeant Pierce gestured at me with his pipe. "Not all criminals are clever."

Frustration rose in me, and heat prickled my skin. Not good, since I was already warm in my coat, and Sergeant Pierce's office had a small heater going to keep out the damp chill. "What about Rosie and our unknown man?"

He shrugged. "They're suspects too. Let's say Charlotte wanted to get even with a john or another prostitute. Maybe she had a grudge against her madam."

"Against Edna? Unlikely. Besides, women are more apt to poison their victims, not eviscerate them."

Sergeant Pierce repacked his pipe and lit it. I waited, sitting on the edge of my chair. The detective in me knew he was right, but the human part of me wanted to believe Charlotte was innocent. "True, but if she had help..."

There was no point in staying. I stood and went to the door. On the threshold, I turned to him. "Charlotte's innocent. You'll see."

***

"Jack the Ripper a father?" Stephen shook his head. "I don't like it."

Neither did I. But why murder his daughter? For that matter, why kill Madge and Olivia?

Even more frustrating, I couldn't tie Madge in with the other two girls, at least not by relation.

"At any rate, I'm glad you're safe." Stephen placed his hand on my knee, and squeezed gently. "I don't know what I'd do if I lost you."

I leaned against him, his body warm. Vampires were supposed to be cold, lifeless entities? If so, Stephen and I were anomalies. He'd told me we were what would be considered "living vampires," those who drank blood but hadn't died.

Which was why religious symbols didn't deter us, and we didn't sleep in coffins filled with graveyard dirt. Sensitivity to the sun was simply the result of a physiological change.

"Don't worry," I assured him, massaging his thigh in return. "I've no plans to let the Ripper kill me."

"Our friend seems to have made himself scarce. Maybe he's left the city."

I leaned back against the chesterfield. "I don't think so." Once we found the elusive Rosie, we'd likely find the Ripper as well.

This meant another trip to the tenements to talk to Rachel.

Stephen's hand moved up my leg. "Any ideas where to look?"

Heat rose in my face and chest. This was a pleasurable feeling and my stomach tightened. Stephen was doing his best to distract me.

"Not really," I admitted. "He'll stay away from places where he can be recognized."

Stephen nodded, finger idly tracing circles on my thigh.

I shifted, my pants tight.

"You weren't planning on going anywhere, were you?" he asked, leaning in and nuzzling my neck. "Not right away, I mean."

"I don't think I could if I wanted."

He reached behind me to rub the back of my neck while nuzzling my throat, breath tickling sensitive skin.

I gave a contented sigh.

"I could stay like this forever," he murmured.

"Do you want to drink?"

He pulled back. His incisors had already dropped. My own followed, and I licked my lips in anticipation.

"What about you?" he asked.

His breath on my neck stirred my own bloodlust.

We'd learned to read each other's physical signals. Looking into Stephen's eyes, I could see desire stirring within their depths. The need to pleasure him, to bring him to the brink of ecstasy made my groin tighten and I leaned into him. My body ached for release, every nerve charged. Stephen leaned his head back. I bit his throat.

The pulsing of his artery counterpointed to each swallow as I drank. I placed my hand over his heart, feeling each beat under my palm.

Stephen's fingers traced my neckline from jaw to throat. I tensed, the sharp point of a nail cutting into my flesh.

I pulled back, licking droplets of blood from my upper lip. Seconds later, Stephen leaned into me. His fangs punctured my neck, and he began to feed.

Several minutes later, he gave a contented sigh, and released me.

"I don't ever want to lose you," he said again.

"You won't." I traced my bite marks on his neck with a delicate finger.

A look of desperation crossed his face. "You don't understand. It's more than just the bonding. I can't stand to lose you."

This was the closest he'd ever come to saying, "I love you." I traced the contour of his mouth with my index finger. "You won't. I promise. We'll always be together."

Stephen took my finger and nipped the tip. Pleasurable feelings stirred through me again as he licked the wound clean.

He could be very persuasive. It only took a glance from him to the stairs for me to nod, readily agreeing.

I'd visit Rosie's mother tonight. The bar could remain closed for a couple of hours.

Chapter Eleven

Thanks to Francis, I didn't have to close the bar. He must've seen a look on my face that told him not to remove his apron when I entered the bar.

Either that or he was used to my idiosyncrasies.

"I'm going out," I told him, "but I should be back within a couple of hours."

Francis rolled his eyes. "You need to bring Stephen with you. That way he can watch the bar while you run around doing Lord knows what."

I grinned. "Can you really see Stephen serving customers?"

He thought for a moment. "No," he said as he shook his head. "The day that happens, I'll think Judgment Day is nigh." His tone turned serious. "Have the police found Charlotte?"

I told him Charlotte's fate. "Sergeant Pierce seems reluctant to release her."

"Surely he doesn't think she's the killer?" Francis shook his head, blond tufts rising and falling.

"Unfortunately, yes." I poured a shot of whiskey. "I gave him some information I came across. Hopefully, he'll use it."

"You can't leave investigating alone, can you? You are no longer a DI." Francis reached for my empty glass. He held up the whiskey bottle. "Another?"

"No, thank you. I'd better be going."

"Good luck."

"Thanks. I'll probably need it."

Leaving Francis to deal with customers, I headed toward the tenements. I hoped Rachel was willing to answer a few questions.

A black wreath hung on Rachel's door.

Trepidation filled me, and I wiped damp palms on my trousers. What'd happened? Visions of a mutilated Rosie flashed through my mind, and I prayed she hadn't become the Ripper's latest victim.

I had to knock twice before Rosie's mother opened the door. She gave me a dour look, eyes red-rimmed and glassy. She'd been crying.

"Whaddya want?" Her words slurred, and I smelled whiskey on her breath.

"To extend my condolences."

She glanced at the wreath. "Well, you have. Now shove off wi' you."

She started to shut the door. I put my foot in the way. "Wait! I need to talk to you about Rosie."

Rachel glared at me and spat. "Don't talk to me about *her*. No daughter of mine would let her little brother get run o'er by a tram. Insolent little ingrate!"

Her grief-filled anger caused her to back away a step. It was enough. I pushed the door open a little more. Rachel continued to glower, but allowed me to enter.

The interior was dim, lit only by an oil lamp. The air was filled with the odors of boiled cabbage, whiskey, and tears. A child's porcelain doll sat on a window sill awaiting its owner's return. A crack marred its face, and one glass eye was missing.

Rachel collapsed in a torn wicker chair. She started to reach for the whiskey bottle on the table, but stopped. Instead, she twisted her hands in her lap.

"When did this happen?" I asked.

She sniffled into her apron before looking at me, tears staining her face.

"He didn't have to do it! Robert never did nothing to him. She let him do it!"

"Who? Rosie's father?" I hoped she would divulge information that could help me.

She gave me a look, then blew her nose on the hem of her dress. "How'd you know about the likes of 'im?"

"Rosie was friends with a girl named Amelia. They were half-sisters. Same father, different mothers." I pulled out a cigarette case, and offered her a smoke. She took it with trembling fingers. "How did you meet him?"

She put the cigarette between her lips, and went to the stove, where she pulled a box of wood matches from a shelf. She struck one, lit her cigarette, and handed the box to me.

I lit my smoke and watched her. Somehow, this simple act seemed to calm her.

"I wasn't always like this." Rachel gave me a defiant look as if challenging me to contradict her. "Before Rosie was born, I was governess for a businessman and his family. They moved to London and took me with them."

Blowing smoke heavenward, I waited for her to continue.

"But the master's wife was jealous. Turned me out while he was on one of his trips. I wandered the streets until he, Rosie's father, that is, found me. Offered me a place to stay, a meal..." Rachel tapped ashes onto a saucer, a dreamy, faraway look in her eyes. "I was young, believed his every word..." She fell silent. "He gave me money to return home when he found out." Rosie's mother looked at me. "Then one day, Rosie tells me another girl says he's her father, too." She turned away, a bitter expression on her face. "Rosie got it in her head he liked his other daughter better. Maybe that's why she ran away."

I leaned forward in my chair, anticipation spiraling through me. Would I finally learn the Ripper's identity? "What was his name?"

She gave me an annoyed look as she drew another drag on her cigarette. "I don't remember. She leaned back and stared at the ceiling. "Maybe I don't want to remember."

I nodded, hoping she didn't sense my disappointment. Maybe she had forgotten his name. She seemed to want to forget the memories. "And you think Rosie's with him?"

Rachel rolled her eyes. "Are you daft? Of course she's with him! Didn't I just tell you they killed my little boy?" She hugged herself, knees pulled up to her chin. "Then there's that time..." Her voice trailed off.

"That time?" I encouraged her.

She gave me a sidelong glance. "No, you wouldn't believe it. The newspapers talk 'bout it, but you know they don't believe their own words."

"The dogs?" I ventured.

Rachel drew another drag on her cigarette. "Aye, but it's not dogs. No, sir. A wolf. Big, shaggy, amber eyes. And my Rosie standing next to it as brave as you please." She shook her head. "Saw it wi' me own eyes. I did. That girl's in league with the Devil, she is."

I didn't dispute that. But what did Rosie hope to gain by her alliance with Jack the Ripper?

I bowed. "My condolences on the loss of your son."

"Thank you. If you see my daughter, tell her she's no longer welcomed here."

"Yes, ma'am." I didn't tell her Rosie would likely never return home.

Walking back to The Cloak and Dagger, I tried to think of a motive Rosie would have for helping her father murder her half-sister and brother. I figured Amelia's murder to be nothing more than jealousy – a need to eliminate the competition. Amelia was the prettier daughter and probably favored by her father. Yet Rosie had convinced the Ripper to murder Amelia, or, she had killed her.

Why Robert? Most likely a situation of being in the wrong place at the wrong time.

I still had more questions than answers when I entered the saloon. Francis looked relieved to see me. I couldn't say I blamed him, considering the size of the crowd.

"You wouldn't believe what they're talking about," Francis said as he untied his apron.

"Try me." I reached for my smock. "I don't think anything could surprise me."

"A wolf." Francis shrugged into his coat. "Rumor says there's a wolf loose 'round this part of the city."

"I suppose it's feasible." I gathered the few glasses left on the bar. "We are surrounded by wilderness."

"But a wolf in the city?" Francis gave a derisive snort. "They're normally afraid of humans."

"Have there been any attacks?"

"Not that I am specifically aware of."

"Maybe it wasn't a wolf, but a Siberian Husky."

Francis seemed to consider that theory. "True." He looked around the room. "I heard the men talk about how they're going to ask the Mayor to impose a curfew and keep themselves armed in case it comes back."

"Are you sure this isn't an attempt by the temperance union to make sure no one can get a drink or spend time with a young lady of the night?"

He quirked an eyebrow. "I never thought of that."

"Not only would we lose business, but this talk of a wolf might cause unnecessary panic."

"I understand what you mean, sir." Francis donned his Homburg. "I won't say a word to anyone. Anyway, I don't believe there's a wolf."

Perhaps he didn't, but from the murmurs of agitated conversation around me, it seemed many customers did. And their resolve to stop this wolf intensified with the more beer and whiskey they drank.

I didn't argue with them, didn't engage in any of the ongoing debates. I stood behind the counter, jotting notes on a piece of paper while the men argued and challenged one another.

Rosie's mother had been a governess, forced out of a job and into a life of poverty in the tenements. Had she ever told Rosie about her father?

Had both daughters been able to shape shift? What if one could, but the other couldn't? Could this be a motive for murder?

The more I thought about it, the more I could connect Rosie and the Ripper to Amelia's murder, even Robert's. Madge's death was the only anomaly.

Later that night, after assuring some of my concerned patrons I could protect myself in the event of a wolf attack, I decided to close the bar early to search for this elusive creature.

Because if I found Rosie, I'd find the Ripper, and vice versa.

My shoes made no sound on the cobblestones as I walked through the city. Apparently news of the wolf sighting traveled quickly, for very few people were out. A couple of drunks reeled by, clutching each other's arms and singing off key.

I sniffed the air, trying to pick up any wolf smell. Nothing except the overpowering odor of hay and dung, mules and horses.

Perhaps I was going about it all wrong. I'd been concentrating on the tenements, the wharf, the bawdy houses. Maybe the Ripper had grown bored with such prey, and sought wealthier victims, ones he could rob of their spoils.

The thought of him wandering among the rich and affluent of Louisville curdled my stomach. Would he be willing to murder the river city's elite?

The thought nagged at me as I entered the house, still unsatisfied with my inability to make any headway in this investigation.

"Are the Conrads planning any soirees?" I asked Stephen as I entered the foyer.

He took my coat. "We haven't received an invitation, if that's what you're implying."

"Not at all." I followed him into the living room.

Stephen poured me a Scotch and soda. "Why the sudden interest?"

I told him my theory about the Ripper. "What if he thinks he's invincible, and starts targeting the middle and upper classes?"

"I doubt he'd be that foolish."

"How can you be sure?" I took a long swallow of my drink to steady my nerves.

"Not if he wants to end up like Elizabeth of Bathory." Stephen leaned against the fireplace mantel. "She was a Hungarian countess said to bathe in the blood of the peasant girls she tortured and killed." He shrugged. "Not saying the rumors were true. Anyway, that was all right. No one complained. Least of all the girls' families. They knew what could happen to them if they did. But Elizabeth got greedy. Started kidnapping daughters of nobles." He gave me a look. "That didn't set too well, as you can guess." He sat in the armchair. "Do you think the Ripper would be so foolish as to start killing the daughters of the elite families here in the city?"

He had a point. Murder the daughter of a Conrad or Caldwell, and the city's denizens would be ready to hang you without a trial. Cut short the life of a few prostitutes, even push a young boy of the tenements under the wheels of a tram, and no one paid attention.

The Scotch and soda soured in my stomach. "I don't know what to do." Frustrated, I hit the arm of the chesterfield. "I try to think where he might show up next, and I can't even guess."

"There's the chance he may not show up anymore. Most likely, he's not going to overstay his welcome."

I didn't relish the idea of the Ripper moving on to another city and killing more prostitutes. "But this time it's different," I argued. "This time Rosie's with him."

"If you find one, you'll likely find the other."

"I think Rosie got him to kill his other daughter, Amelia. According to Rachel, she saw Rosie and the Ripper together, with him in wolf form, although I doubt she knew it was him. There's the matter of Robert's death. Apparently, Rosie watched her brother get pushed under a mule tram and run over. That's what Rachel said."

"Does she have proof?" Stephen crossed his legs, and leaned back in his chair. His voice was calm, detached, almost as if the murder of a small boy failed to move him. I knew better than to question his callousness. Stephen had seen tortures and death I didn't even want to imagine. He had his way of dealing with pain. Even though he didn't show it, I suspected Robert's death haunted him.

"I'm inclined to believe her. She doesn't have any motive to protect him or Rosie, especially now."

Stephen reached for the humidor and pulled out a cigar. But he didn't light the tobacco-filled cylinder. Instead, he turned it over in his fingers, as if searching for answers in the fibers. "She didn't confront him?"

"I don't think she knows where he is. I think she's afraid of him."

"I see." Stephen rolled the cigar back and forth between his thumb and index finger. "Any witnesses?"

"They probably won't talk to the police. The only one would be the driver, and who knows what state he's in right now."

Stephen gestured with the cigar. "Then that's who we must talk to."

Except we were too late. The next morning, Sergeant Pierce stopped by to tell me the mule tram driver's body had been found floating in the Ohio River, an apparent suicide.

"He was obviously distraught over the accident," Pierce said. "Left a widow."

"Have you talked to Rachel about Rosie and her father?" I asked.

The sergeant shook his head. "Tried to broach the subject and nearly got hit with a bottle."

After giving him my condolences, I accompanied the sergeant to the receiving room. Another promise to let him know if I found any new information and he left, apparently satisfied.

I returned to the living room to find a cup of steaming coffee waiting for me.

"Of course, you don't believe it for a second," Stephen said as he poured his coffee.

I stared at him. "Believe what?"

"That the tram driver took his life." Stephen gave me a direct look over the rim of his cup. "Your detective instincts should be screaming something's wrong."

They were. It was quite feasible the driver would kill himself over grief. However it was more likely the Ripper and Rosie had decided he was a liability, one best eradicated.

"We need to see that body."

"How do you propose we do that?" I didn't have clearance to give the coroner orders, and doubted Sergeant Pierce would intercede for me. "Besides, he's probably already buried."

Another thought came to me, one which chilled my marrow. What about Rachel? She'd accused Rosie and the Ripper of murdering her son. Would they kill her in retaliation?

Damn! I already felt guilty asking Francis to work overtime for me at The Cloak and Dagger. But if I wanted to stop the Ripper, I'd no choice.

Unless...

"I need a favor," I said, praying Stephen wouldn't say no. "I need you to come with me tonight and tend bar while I run a couple of errands." I raised my hand against what I suspected his impending refusal. "I've already asked Francis to cover far too many times for me. It isn't fair to him and I don't want to lose him as an employee."

Stephen lowered his coffee cup. "What do you plan to do?"

"Talk to Sergeant Pierce, for one. But I'm worried about Rachel. I think she may be the Ripper's next victim. I know she won't talk to the police, but he doesn't know that."

Stephen poured himself another cup of coffee. "Wouldn't someone go to the police if they found her body?"

"People who live in the tenements tend to be suspicious of the police," I said. Stephen had never lived in such conditions, so had no notion of such a life. "They think the police are only there to harass them."

"So if something were to happen, no one would talk." Stephen's spoon clinked against the china as he stirred cream and sugar in his coffee.

"Right. They'd refuse to share any information." I crossed my legs and folded my hands atop my knee. "As an investigator, it makes things quite difficult."

Stephen smiled. "I imagine." He pursed his lips, looking at me with a thoughtful expression. "How did you manage?"

I gave him an impetuous smile. "You forget. I used to be a pickpocket vagrant myself."

He rolled his eyes and patted his back pocket. "Thanks for reminding me."

I ignored his jibe. "Point is, I need your help tonight. Poor Francis practically lives at the bar. He needs a well-deserved break." If nothing else, I could appeal to Stephen's sense of duty. Not to mention, he liked Francis.

Several silent seconds passed. I waited, nerves crackling with tension. Finally, Stephen nodded. "I don't like it, but all right."

"Good." I pushed my chair back. "I'm going to bed. Care to join me?"

I knew he wouldn't say no.

Chapter Twelve

Francis looked relieved he could go home at a reasonable hour. But he didn't look convinced while watching Stephen reluctantly tie on a white bartender's apron.

He leaned toward me. "He looks like he'll scare away the customers."

"Do you want to stay and help him?"

That got me a quick shake of his head. "No, thank you. But how'd you manage to persuade him to agree to this?"

"It was either that, or slog through the tenements with me. I convinced him tending bar was easier."

Francis shook his head as he left.

After instructing Stephen on how to pour and mix drinks, and how much to charge, I left him and went to visit Rosie's mother. I planned to stop by the police station afterwards. If things went well, I promised Stephen I'd return in two or three hours.

Surely, he could survive that long.

But, like Francis, Stephen looked even less convinced.

I couldn't help that. Being an investigator, I knew all about being forced out of one's comfort zone. God knows I'd walked across marble floors and slogged through muck and shit. I'd interviewed dirty and uncooperative prostitutes as well as arrested men of social stature. If there was anything my job as a DI had taught me, it was to never second guess or assume where the job would take me.

I'd suspected the Ripper was able to shift into wolf form after the third Whitechapel killing. The reports had always talked about how particular organs, usually female, were missing, but they never went into gruesome detail of how the bodies were ripped and mangled. The Ripper probably removed the organs after shifting back to human form.

If I'd revealed my suspicions to my superiors, I would've been locked away in Bedlam. Working in an unofficial capacity proved beneficial. True, I had to go through official channels. I was restricted as to what evidence I was permitted to see, but there were no superiors to report to, no paperwork to fill out.

Tonight there were a few people on the streets. Apparently, the absence of any further murders, and no recent wolf or feral dog sightings, had convinced some there was no longer any danger walking the streets at night.

An old woman, smelling of cabbage and potatoes, sat on the stoop in front of Rachel's house. Her chin touched her ample chest. She looked up at the crunch of my footsteps on the cobblestones.

"Lord, bad times fall on this house." Like Rosie's mother, she was missing her front teeth.

Even though I'd suspected, that familiar sense of dread washed over me. "She's dead."

The old woman nodded. "We heard her screams. Saw that wolf, too. Big it 'twas." She tugged a crucifix from beneath her black smock. "Devil dog. Some say if you see it, you'll die in a year." She gave me a knowing look. "I've made my peace wit' God, if you know what I mean."

I nodded, and started past her to the door. The black wreath still hung on the nail, except now it was tattered and falling apart, a toy discarded by the elements. "Have you called the police?"

Her mocking laugh followed me. "What're they gonna do? Their guns can't kill the devil."

The door to Rachel's apartment was cracked. I pushed it open, the malodorous stench of decay and old blood heavy in the air. Pulling out a handkerchief, I covered my mouth and nose.

She lay on the floor between the stove and table. Blood had soaked through her dress and apron, dyeing both a dark rusty color. From her throat down to her abdomen, long vicious claw marks raked her skin, rending flesh from muscle.

I knelt by the corpse. Using my handkerchief, I lifted an arm. Scratches crossed her palms, defensive wounds. Rigor mortis had recently set in.

There was no need to look for fingerprints.

Except for an overturned chair, nothing else seemed disturbed. A Bible lay on the table, open to Psalms 21. Rachel must've been trying to console herself over the death of Robert.

I stepped outside, closing the door behind me. The old woman was gone. Perhaps satisfied someone had come, she no longer felt any obligation to stay.

At the police station, I told Sergeant Pierce about finding Rachel's body, and how I suspected the Ripper or Rosie had murdered her and Robert. When I mentioned the animal scratches, he raised his hand and nodded.

"I shouldn't tell you this, but we found similar marks on the body of that tram driver."

My suspicions were correct. He'd been mauled to death, then dumped in the Ohio River.

"What about Rosie? Have you found her?"

He shook his head. "If she's involved, she's keeping quiet."

"If you know it's the Ripper and possibly Rosie, why keep Charlotte locked up?"

Sergeant Pierce swung his booted feet off his desk and onto the floor with a heavy clomp. He gave me an exasperated look. "She didn't tell you? A young woman bailed her out. They left together."

"Who was she?"

He shrugged. "Probably one of Big Edna's girls. The madam would have the money."

Despite my reluctance, I had to admit he could be right. I couldn't help but feel something was amiss as I walked back to The Cloak and Dagger. This feeling intensified as I drew closer, but for another reason. Strident voices and the sound of crashing furniture disturbed the otherwise quiet street.

A bar fight? Bloody hell. I burst inside to see Stephen looming over the bar, face dark with rage. In each fist, he held the shirt collars of a couple of drunks. From his flexed muscles, I suspected he intended to throw them over his shoulders and across the room.

His vampiric strength would make it as easy as tossing paper balls.

His anger could also unwittingly make his fangs drop and reveal his true nature.

I slammed the door. Hard. The building trembled. Someone dropped a glass. The resounding crash made a few jump, nerves already on edge.

I strode through the rapidly parting crowd. Grabbing the back of the men's shirt collars, I yanked them out of Stephen's grip. They landed on their butts. Staring up at me with wide eyes, both drunks scrabbled backward like crabs.

I ignored them and turned to Stephen. "What the hell is going on?"

He glared, and threw down the bar towel. "I told them they'd had too much to drink and they decided to argue with me."

I studied the two men. Not regulars. They'd moved to a table while watching me with baleful eyes. They were ready to fight at the slightest provocation.

I came to their table, and loomed over it, palms planted on the surface. Although I hadn't noticed before, the odor of whiskey wafted from their sullen mouths.

"Gentlemen, I see you're new here. I'm the owner. Let me be the first to tell you the rules. If my bartender says you've had enough, you've had enough."

"Sorry," one said, voice surly.

I straightened. "You're welcome to stay. But cause any more trouble, and I'll toss you both out myself." The grin I gave them made them shrink back. "Are we in agreement?"

Their heads bobbed up and down. I patted them each on the shoulder, and made my way to the bar. Tying on my apron, I gave Stephen an exasperated look.

"I can't take you anywhere!" I snatched the towel he'd dropped, and began wiping glasses. "Two hours. That's all I asked for you to stay out of trouble. And you can't?"

Stephen leaned against the bar and crossed his arms over his chest. "I'm not used to dealing with the likes of dregs like those."

I resisted the urge to roll my eyes. "As if they're used to dealing with you. Don't you think exhibiting such a show of strength might look suspicious?" I turned away, placing the glasses in their proper place. Looking around the room, I noticed how unnaturally quiet it was, many of the men sipping their beers while staring at Stephen with wary eyes.

I turned to him. "All right. You can go. I'll handle it from here."

Stephen gave me a suspicious look. "Are you sure?"

"Who's been working here? You or me? And don't be looking for trouble on the way home."

He inclined his head toward the two drunks, who continued to glare at us. "What about them?"

Sitting and glaring was legal. But it was the way the men sat, tense, as if ready to suddenly uncoil and strike like a snake that bothered me. Nevertheless, I couldn't show any fear or concern. To do so might convince them to try something foolish, like start a fight. And while I had no concerns about myself or Stephen, I saw no need to involve other customers.

They watched Stephen pass on his way to the door. Hopefully, his leaving would pacify them. The tavern would go back to normal.

But when I looked over a few minutes later, the men were no longer there.

I looked around the room, thinking perhaps they'd moved elsewhere. Foreboding filled me. Maybe I was being paranoid, but I couldn't help but feel those men had followed Stephen.

Not that I worried about my lover. But I'd fought drunks in my youth. Often, lack of reason compelled them to commit violent acts they might not have otherwise.

They might discover a hangover to be the least of their problems if they picked a fight with Stephen.

Conversations began humming around me. Many of the men seemed at ease, now that the tension in the room had abated. I kept quiet. My job was to serve drinks, not opinions. I always tried to remain neutral and never take sides. It was another lesson I'd learned from my work as a DI. Allow yourself to see only one side of an issue and you risked being unable to solve the case.

Unfortunately, my colleagues at Scotland Yard would never believe the Ripper was a wolf shifter. And that hindered their investigation, allowing him to escape.

At last, it was closing time. I'd phoned Stephen several times, but received no answer. Strange. My stomach tightened with apprehension. What if he'd attacked the two men and been arrested? But Sergeant Pierce would've told me. Where was he?

Outside, in my impatience to lock the door to The Cloak and Dagger, I dropped my key on the cobblestones. Icy chills snaked up my spine as I bent down to retrieve it.

I turned to see someone, who could only be Rosie, staring at me. Her blue-gray eyes regarded me without emotion. She wore a lavender dress and a long shawl that might've been white once upon a time but was now dingy with dust and grime. Black hair fell in tumbled curls around her face. We stared at each other for several seconds. I think she looked right through as if she never saw me. Then, as if hearing a noise I couldn't, she turned and ran down the street, hair and shawl billowing behind her.

I debated giving chase. Perhaps she could lead me to the Ripper. But there was still the question of what had happened to Stephen.

Frustrated, I shoved the key in the lock and twisted it. Too bad vampire abilities didn't include being in two places at once.

She had headed downtown. Maybe toward the tenements or Edna's or Annabelle's bawdy houses. After struggling with my conscience, I decided to head home, my concern for Stephen overriding my desire to investigate Rosie's whereabouts. Once I knew Stephen was all right, I'd head downtown, and see if I could find any clues.

I was about four blocks from home when I saw them. My heart plummeted, hitting the ground and exploding in a gush of disbelief and horror. I staggered back, bile rising in my throat, and pressed my hand against my nose and mouth. Taking a deep breath, I ordered myself not to vomit.

The two drunks dangled like macabre scarecrows on the spikes of a wrought iron fence. Their throats had been slashed, torsos ripped open, guts hanging loose, glinting with grease and fat in the glow of a gas light. A large pool of blood coagulated on the cobblestones.

I ran home, denial pounding in my brain in counterpoint to the slapping of my soles on the pavement.

No! No! No! Oh, God, Stephen, why? My hands clenched into fists as I tried to push the gruesome images out of my mind.

How could he have done this?

Anger filled me, and I nearly wrenched the doorknob off.

He met me in the foyer. I stormed past him into the living room.

"Is everything all right?" he asked, voice filled with concern.

I wanted to grab him by the shirt collar, throttle him, scream and demand to know why he'd killed those men. I wanted to hate him and myself for trusting a monster like him, a demonic being now showing his true face. Instead, I sank into the upholstered chair, and put my head in my hands. If Stephen was what I'd become, I wanted to die now.

Stephen didn't approach me. Considering my rage, it was probably a wise decision.

"What happened?"

I stared at him, fingers pressed against my temples. "You don't know? Or are you in denial?" I paused. Maybe he wasn't aware. Maybe in a fit of rage, he'd blacked out.

I didn't know my lover as well as I thought, even after ten years.

Did this mean I didn't know myself?

He looked hurt at my accusation. His brow furrowed. "No, I'm sorry, but I don't."

I placed my hands on my knees and drew a deep breath. "Those two men who assaulted you in the bar. They followed you, didn't they?"

Stephen nodded. "But you figured they would, right?"

"Yes."

"Did something happen to them?"

I told him, my voice dispassionate. Funny how the deaths of the prostitutes and Rosie's mother had not garnered the same reaction from me as the murders of the two drunks.

But that was because the man I loved, or thought I loved, was possibly their killer. The one person I trusted was possibly betraying me.

He shook his head when I'd finished. "I can't believe you would think that." Pain, anger, and frustration filled his voice. "You really think I'm capable of doing that knowing how your sister died?"

Guilt overwhelmed me. Now, sitting here, talking to him, I realized how foolish my initial thoughts had been. Stephen never killed indiscriminately.

But if he hadn't killed them, who had?

My stomach roiled. The Ripper. Somehow, he'd followed Stephen and murdered the men.

A chill washed over me. Did he know where we lived? Would he try to kill us during daylight, when he had the advantage?

Stephen headed for the front door.

"Where are you going?" I asked.

"I want to see those bodies. Maybe we can find a clue."

I hurried after him, apprehension making my legs tremble. I'd no desire to see those mangled corpses again.

"Show me where the bodies are," he said.

I pointed down the street. "There."

We drew closer, gaslight lamps casting our shadows long across the cobblestones.

"Where?" Stephen asked.

Impatient, I jabbed my index finger at the iron fence. "There!"

My arm dropped to my side, and my mouth fell open.

There were no bodies, no pools of blood. No sign of murder.

Chapter Thirteen

I stared at Stephen, unable to correlate what I'd seen and what I now saw.

"It was here." I examined the fence for blood stains, torn clothing, hair, any evidence.

Stephen arched his eyebrow. "Whatever it was, it's gone now."

But I'd seen the men impaled and mangled.

If it'd been my imagination, had I imagined Rosie?

He placed a hand on my shoulder. "Let's go back."

I nodded. Right now we would only draw attention to ourselves standing in the middle of an empty street. Better to go home and try to sort this out later. All I wanted was to sleep.

Stephen seemed to understand my anxiety. He curled up behind me on the bed, one arm thrown protectively over my chest. I breathed in his smell, comforted by the fact he was still mine, still safe.

And not a killer.

***

I don't know how long I slept, but when I awoke, Stephen was already up. From the murmur of voices, mingling with the luscious smell of brewing coffee, it sounded like we had a visitor.

I dressed quickly and went downstairs. Sergeant Pierce sat on the chesterfield. He rose upon seeing me, holding a cup of coffee on a saucer. He wore his uniform, but whether he was on his way to work, or returning home, I couldn't say.

"What brings you here?" I poured myself a cup from the coffeepot on the sideboard.

"I wanted to ask you about Rachel's death."

"What did you want to talk to me about?"

"We found hairs on the body. But not human hairs. Coarser."

"Like that of a wolf?"

He gave me a penetrating look. "They could be hairs of a dog."

"But you know it isn't." I sat on the sofa and put my cup on the coffee table. "Wolf hairs are different from dogs'."

Sergeant Pierce placed his cup and saucer on the fireplace mantle. "But why and how would a wolf attack someone in their home?"

"Maybe it's a werewolf." I gave a weak laugh, hoping I sounded like I was making the comment in jest. "Another Peter Stubbe."

"Who?" He looked confused, and, from his narrowed eyes, concerned about my mental state.

"A serial killer from the sixteenth century. His accusers claimed he was a werewolf. He was tortured before finally being killed, his head impaled on a pike."

"You English and your criminal justice system."

"It happened in Germany."

Sergeant Pierce waved a dismissive hand. "A werewolf? It's certainly a novel idea, but only as that, a story."

I sipped my coffee. "Do you have any other theories? Besides the possibility it's a dog?" A thought came to me. "Maybe it's an orangutan like in Poe's *Murder in the Rue Morgue*."

He looked unhappy. "You're teasing me."

"Sorry." Yes indeed I was. Just because I had knowledge about the Ripper that Sergeant Pierce didn't – knowledge I wanted to share – didn't mean I needed to make his job difficult. "Perhaps the killer takes a dog with him." The only way I could prove Jack the Ripper was a werewolf was to have the sergeant with me when the Ripper shifted.

Only problem was I didn't know when that would be.

"Have you seen any dog near the bodies?" Sergeant Pierce asked. "We've been interviewing people in the neighborhoods where the attacks took place, but no one's admitted to seeing anything."

I debated telling him what the old woman and Rachel had told me. But I wanted to keep that knowledge to myself a little longer, see if my theory was right. "They probably won't," I said. "For one, they're not going to make the connection. For another, if it's in the tenements, they'd probably chase it away. Competition for food."

"You're probably right." Sergeant Pierce reached for his patrol cap. "If you hear or see anything, let me know." It wasn't a question.

"Of course." I walked him to the door. "Good luck."

"I'll need it," he admitted glumly.

I closed the door to the foyer and listened to the front door open and close. If Sergeant Pierce didn't believe in werewolves, what would he have thought if I'd revealed my fangs during his visit?

Stephen came into the living room. "Getting desperate, are we?"

"What do you mean?"

"Dropping hints about a werewolf being the killer." Stephen took Sergeant Pierce's cup and saucer, and headed toward the kitchen. He turned back on the threshold. "You don't really think he believes in the supernatural, do you?"

"He'll have to if he wants to find the killer." I poured myself another cup of coffee.

Stephen shook his head. "Keep drinking that, and it'll be coffee coursing through your veins instead of blood."

"Very funny." I raised the cup toward him. "Stop making it so perfect, and maybe I will quit."

He gave me a mischievous smirk. "Dare me?"

"You do," I warned, "and not only will I refuse to drink your blood, I'll dismiss you."

"Evict me from my own home?" Stephen didn't look contrite when he went into the kitchen.

***

I had to admit to feeling relieved when I saw Charlotte sitting at the bar in The Cloak and Dagger. Her face looked pinched and her hair was in disarray, but she was free.

Unfortunately, the threat of a trial still loomed.

She and Francis had been talking as I entered the bar. Seeing me, Charlotte practically bowled me over with an enthusiastic hug.

"Nathan! I missed you!"

"I missed you, too." I gently extricated her arms from around my neck. Charlotte was strong despite her small size. I held her hands and looked her up and down. Today, she wore a black skirt and white shirtwaist. "You look much better."

She beamed. "Thank you."

Francis spoke up. "She told me about the knife. Sounds like a set up."

I nodded, guiding Charlotte back to the bar. "Do you have any idea who might've tried to implicate you?" I poured her a shot of brandy.

She drained the glass in one gulp. "To be honest, no. I get along with the other girls, even the ones who work at Annabelle's."

"Do any of them know you were in jail on murder charges?"

She rolled the edge of the shot glass back and forth on the bar. "I don't think so. Edna came by the jail, but she promised she wouldn't tell the others."

That meant one of Edna's girls hadn't bailed her out. Apparently, Edna wanted this scandal kept quiet. "You shouldn't go back out on the streets. At least not until we can find this killer."

Charlotte raised her glass. "I appreciate your concern, but a lady likes to earn her own keep." She gave Francis a seductive look over the rim of her glass. I assumed her words hit the target from the way his fingers clenched the bar towel as he wiped his wine glass.

I understood how he felt. When I'd experienced the first stirrings of attraction toward Stephen, I'd worried he'd reject me at best, or beat and kill me at worst. We lived in an atmosphere of fear despite Jeremy Bentham's call for the decriminalization of homosexuality. Even the celebrated Oscar Wilde had found himself in jail on charges of "gross indecency." If a famous author wasn't safe, what chance did we have?

The moral groups frowned on what they considered debauchery, a relationship between a man and a woman was preferred to that of one between two men. It wasn't fair, and I didn't like it, but we had no choice.

Francis folded the towel over a rail. "Charlotte, if you like I'll escort you home."

She squeezed his upper arm and kissed his cheek. "I'll stop by your house later. I want to talk to Nathan."

Francis gave her a dejected smile and left, head down, shoulders slumped.

The bar was quieter than usual. I took advantage of this opportunity to ask Charlotte some questions.

"How's business?"

She shrugged. "The murders seem to have stopped."

"Of prostitutes. Now they include a small boy, a mother, and a tram driver."

Her eyes widened. "The same killer?"

"Sergeant Pierce thinks the murderer takes a dog with him and the dog attacks the victims."

"It would make sense." Charlotte reached for the brandy bottle. "Did you find that missing girl? Rosie?"

"Yes, and it's only created more problems. It was her mother and brother who were murdered."

She gave a long, low whistle. "Have you talked to her? Maybe she knows something."

Part of me wanted to tell Charlotte the truth, but a good detective never gives away all of his information. "Unfortunately, we don't know her whereabouts. She's disappeared again." I decided to change the subject. "What do you know about Madge? Do you know if she had any connection to Amelia? Like a family relation?"

Drink poured, she replaced the bottle. "Not that I know of. Madge was a strange one. She told me she wanted to be a nun."

I overfilled a customer's glass. "A nun?" Snatching the towel, I wiped beer and foam from the bar and my hand.

Charlotte shrugged thin shoulders. "I know. How does one go from wanting to be a nun to being a whore?" She smoothed her skirt and ran her fingers through her hair, as if remembering her job was attracting men.

"Circumstances can change people's purposes."

"No one faulted her religious beliefs," Charlotte continued. "She seemed sincere. Went to Mass every day, wore a rosary. She invited us to join her." She gave me a sad smile. "We always refused. Politely, of course. No need to hurt her feelings. Of course, we wondered what the parishioners thought, if they knew who she really was."

Difficult as it was to be a vampire, I couldn't imagine trying to live one kind of life while wishing for another. I'd made my decision when I realized the Ripper wasn't human and would need preternatural powers to stop him.

But why would the Ripper kill a girl for her religious yearnings? That didn't fit his modus operandi. Then again, neither did killing young boys, their mothers, and tram drivers.

Charlotte raised an index finger. "I do remember something. This Rosie, I told you she was part of our company?"

"Yes."

"She and Madge got into this argument once about Black Monday. Rosie said Catholics were evil because they worshipped the Virgin Mary, and Irish Catholics were the worst."

"Madge was Irish?"

Charlotte shrugged. "I don't know. But Madge became very upset. Turned white, started shaking. She told Rosie she'd rot in hell for saying that."

The situation was starting to make sense. "What did Rosie do?"

She frowned, remembering. "It was the strangest reaction. She merely smiled and walked away. No one said anything and, eventually, we forgot about it."

Someone hadn't. "Who was there?"

"Let's see." Charlotte ticked the names off her fingers. "Me, Madge, Rosie, and Olivia."

If what Charlotte said was true, Rosie most likely planned to kill her, since she'd witnessed the altercation. No motive but vengeance. Like her father, Rosie seemed to enjoy murder for murder's sake.

I poured us each a snifter of brandy. I didn't want to scare her. Not that Charlotte frightened easily. I'd no doubt she could defend herself. But a fight against a werewolf, possibly two? She could act as brave as she wanted, but it wouldn't help.

I replenished a customer's drink, then returned to her. "Tell me about the knife."

Charlotte tucked a strand of hair behind her ear. "I already told Sergeant Pierce. I was walking down the street when someone grabbed me from behind, and pushed a nasty smelling rag over my face. I blacked out. I woke up in an alley with the knife in my hand. A policeman stood over me." She threw up her hands. "Next thing I know, I'm arrested for possible murder." She shook her head in disgust. "And the police wonder why we don't help them."

"I'm sure you'll be exonerated."

She patted my hand. "Thank you."

"Who posted your bail?"

She mulled over that question. "I'm not sure. She said she worked for Big Edna, but I never saw her before. Blonde-haired girl. After she took me back to the brothel, she disappeared."

Had Big Edna sent the blonde, or was someone else responsible for Charlotte's bail? Posting bond also meant making sure the bonded party returned to court. If Rosie had helped Charlotte, why? Wouldn't she have just killed her? Or did she intend to make sure Charlotte stood trial? But why not keep her in jail?

"What are you thinking?" Charlotte asked.

"Nothing." I squeezed her hand. "I'm glad you're safe."

She pressed back. "So am I."

The rest of the night we played cards, and Charlotte even consented to play the piano and sing a couple of raucous tavern tunes for those regulars who insisted they missed her.

Closing time finally came. Charlotte grabbed her wrap and followed me outside.

I locked the door, and we set off for Francis's house. He lived in a shotgun dwelling on the west side.

He sat on his front stoop, cigarette dangling from his mouth. Seeing us approach, he removed the smoke, and ground it out on the cobblestones.

"I promised I'd deliver her safe and sound." I gave Charlotte a chaste kiss on the cheek. "See you tomorrow night. Be good."

"Promise." She returned the kiss, then went inside with Francis.

What they decided to do once that door closed was their prerogative. I turned and headed home, taking an available mule tram part way. I wanted to hurry and be with Stephen.

Too bad I couldn't stop worrying about Charlotte.

***

The next morning found Stephen's warm breath tickling the hairs on the back of my neck. I cracked open bleary eyes and sat up, careful not to disturb him. Looking down on his long, lean form under the sheet, I resisted the urge to kiss his shoulder.

He didn't resist the urge to moan, roll over, and drape his arm across me.

"You're not asleep," I said.

"No," he mumbled, eyes still closed.

I took his hand, placed it against my carotid artery. "Neither am I."

Stephen opened his eyes and looked at me. "Demanding, aren't you?"

He sat up, pushing me against the headboard. Our mouths met in a demanding kiss, tongues intertwining. He nipped at my lower lip, drawing a bead of blood. Leaning back, he licked his lips in anticipation.

"You know I can't resist your blood." His fangs pierced my neck.

I couldn't help myself. I wanted his blood. My groin, abdomen, and thighs tingled with electrical impulses. My fingers tightened around his upper arms, holding him in place. Fangs lowered as desire spiraled through me, and my body started to shake with need. He lifted his head, drops of blood on his lips. Still watching me, he wiped his mouth with his finger and licked it clean.

I placed one hand over his on the bed and leaned in close. Stephen shuddered as I bit at the juncture of his neck and shoulder. Warm blood spurted into my mouth.

He stroked my back as I drank. Sated, I collapsed against the mattress. Several minutes later, I heard low, rhythmic snores.

It was the most beautiful sound I'd ever heard.

***

The day passed uneventfully. Stephen and I played chess or read. Neither of us talked about the Ripper, murders, or werewolves.

After a brief nap, I called Francis.

"Hello?" He sounded harried.

"Is everything all right?" I clutched the receiver, hoping I'd only interrupted a tryst between him and Charlotte.

Silence. "Is Charlotte with you?"

The receiver slipped from my hand, and I scrambled to catch it before it hit the floor. "No, she isn't."

I heard a muffled curse, and sagged against the wall.

"Charlotte's missing."

Chapter Fourteen

Francis had been drying the same glass for ten minutes. He looked haggard, dark circles under his eyes, hair an unruly mess. Like he hadn't slept all night. And he probably hadn't.

"After we..." He gestured vaguely with his hand and gave me a look.

"Please continue."

"I fell asleep. She must've left sometime in the early morning. There was a note saying she'd gone to see you."

"And you didn't suspect anything?"

Francis set the glass on the bar, and gave me a long-suffering look. "I'm a bartender, not an inspector like you were."

"Of course. You'd no reason to believe she'd lie."

"I should've looked for her. But I thought she'd come back." He gave me a remorseful look. "Sergeant Pierce won't be happy about this, will he?"

"You let me handle him." Francis wasn't in any shape to deal with customers judging from the dejected look on his face and the slow way he moved.

I phoned Stephen, asked if Charlotte had stopped by. He informed me she hadn't.

Part of me wanted to close the bar and search for her. Had she been kidnapped? Run away? Although I couldn't imagine Charlotte doing such a thing, visions of her mangled body crossed my mind, and I pushed them aside, annoyed at my lack of focus.

I called Stephen again. He reluctantly agreed to join us, provided I didn't make him serve drinks.

I told him this was too important, but didn't give any details. Under the pretext of feeling ill, I convinced my customers I needed to close the tavern early, with a promise I'd try to reopen the next day. When one of them suggested Francis stay, I told him his wife was near to having her baby, and he needed to be with her.

It was a lie, but a very effective one.

Stephen arrived within the hour. The brim of his fedora was pulled low over his forehead and the collar of his coat was turned up. Apparently, he didn't want to risk anyone recognizing him.

Along with Francis, I outlined my plan. I'd report the incident to Sergeant Pierce, then talk to Edna and Annabelle. Francis would see if he could pick up Charlotte's trail. Stephen would search the tenements.

"We'll meet back here in three hours." Both Stephen and Francis had keys to the tavern, in case they returned before I did.

We went our separate ways. At the police station, Sergeant Pierce ushered me into his office.

I told him about Charlotte's disappearance.

"Had a feeling that would happen." He lit his pipe.

"What do you mean?"

He gave me a look from over top of his pipe bowl. "I can't believe you haven't figured it out. Of all people, I thought you would."

"Excuse me." I felt a little peevish myself. "I've given you information, and you've waved me off like I'm an idiot. I kept insisting Charlotte was innocent, but you argued she'd been caught with a bloody knife and that was proof enough."

He leaned over the desk toward me, eyes intense, mouth set in a firm line. "Of course she's innocent. I wanted to save her life."

I nearly fell off my chair. "What?"

He pulled out a file filled with photographs of the victims, interviews, and his reports. "Charlotte is the only one of a group of young ladies who, with the exception of this Rosie, were murdered. She told me what'd happened between Madge and Rosie." He closed the file and put it on the desk. "Question is, would Rosie have murdered them if her father hadn't arrived?"

"Rosie was said to be jealous of her half-sister, Amelia. She killed her because apparently her father favored his other daughter. Then she killed Madge, probably because she said she was going to hell. For the daughter of a killer, that might've seemed too judgmental of an accusation."

"You think Rosie became a murderer to impress her father?"

"It's possible."

He blew a cloud of white smoke into the air. "Plus she and her father were probably responsible for the deaths of her mother, brother, and the tram driver."

My stomach clenched, and I drew a deep breath, not wanting to ask this question, but needing to know. "Do you think she's kidnapped Charlotte?"

"It's very possible." He tapped ashes into the ashtray. The office smelled like Burley field on a cool autumn day. "Don't worry. We'll find them and rescue her. You can rest assured, the Ripper and his daughter won't murder anyone else."

I leaned my head back and stared at the ceiling. His bravado irritated me. I bit my lower lip. Dare I tell him? I'd tried to give him clues, only to sense he didn't believe me. Would he be willing to listen now?

"There's something you need to know about Jack the Ripper, and possibly Rosie."

Again, he gave me that piercing stare. "If you're withholding evidence..."

"No!" I jumped a little, surprised at the tension in my voice. Fingers pressed against the arms of the chair, I took a deep breath. "This is something you've probably not dealt with. But I can assure you, regular bullets won't kill him or his daughter, if it comes to that."

"You make it sound as if he isn't quite human."

My fingernails dug into the palms of my hands. Now or never. But he had to know. Drawing another deep breath, I met his eyes. He had to know this was Nathan James, former Detective Inspector, talking to him, and not Nathan James, owner of The Cloak and Dagger.

Then again, would I've believed him if he told me what I was to say next?

"You're right. The Ripper isn't human. He's a shape shifter, a werewolf. And so, I suspect, is Rosie."

There. I'd said it. I averted my gaze, not wanting to see Sergeant Pierce's face break into a mocking smile. He was probably debating having me committed to the local asylum.

Silence hung heavy in the air. I kept my gaze fixed to the floor, face burning.

He finally spoke, a haze of pipe smoke wafting on the air. "A werewolf?"

"Yes."

"A family of werewolves."

I nodded, still avoiding his gaze. "I think both daughters, Amelia and Rosie, had the ability to shift. But Rosie seemed to take to the idea more." A thought came to me. "Maybe they killed Amelia because she'd become what they detested most rather than out of jealousy."

"But Big Edna said Rosie had also worked briefly as a prostitute."

"That was before the Ripper arrived. She probably never told him. She would kill anyone who revealed her secret."

"Where is he now?" Sergeant Pierce repacked his pipe and lit it.

"I don't know." His lack of concern about the Ripper and Rosie being shifters bothered me, but he didn't confirm or deny my suspicions. I couldn't help but worry he didn't believe me. Still, if anything happened to him or any other officers, I wouldn't forgive myself for not warning them.

The sergeant pushed his chair back. "Look, Nathan, we'll find them. The Ripper may have been lucky in London, but his luck won't last here."

I started to protest, but stopped. I'd said what I had come to say. "You will take what I said into account?"

He clapped a hand on my shoulder as we walked to the door. "I realize you gents at Scotland Yard, indeed all of London, were held in thrall by the Ripper's feats. But over here in America, we'll show you his blood runs as red as yours or mine."

I nodded. I didn't want to think about blood right now. Least of all Charlotte's.

***

Neither Edna nor Annabelle had seen Charlotte. Nor had any of the other prostitutes I asked.

I returned to The Cloak and Dagger first. I wondered how the others were doing as I fixed myself a brandy.

Francis arrived half an hour later. He stamped dirt off his boots before entering. I poured him a Scotch.

"Any luck?"

"None." He sat at the bar and took the glass I offered. "Thank you."

Stephen came in a few minutes later. From the grim look on his face, I gathered he hadn't had any luck, either.

"What did the police say?" Francis asked.

I told them my news. I didn't want to admit I'd confessed to the Ripper being a werewolf, I admitted I'd warned the sergeant.

"And he believed you?" Francis reached for his half-full glass. "It sounds like something out of a penny dreadful."

"I don't know if he believed me or not." I reached for the whiskey bottle.

Francis gave me a sympathetic look. "I don't blame you for wanting to give the police every advantage."

I turned to Stephen. "What about you? Any news?"

He shook his head. This wasn't good. Had the Ripper or Rosie already killed Charlotte?

"What do we do now?" Francis asked.

"Nothing we can do." I drained my glass and set it on the bar. "I suggest we go home. Maybe she'll try to contact us." Apparently, I didn't look convincing because they both gave me suspicious looks.

At the door, Francis looked back at me. "You'll let me know if you find her?"

"Yes."

"You didn't tell Sergeant Pierce about us, did you?" Stephen asked after the door had closed behind Francis.

"Of course not. I wasn't sure I should tell him about the Ripper being a wolf shifter. I'm surprised he didn't have me arrested for public intoxication or committed to an insane asylum." I poured myself another whiskey, fingers shaking. Telling Sergeant Pierce about the Ripper had been the most nerve-wracking thing I'd ever done. One that could jeopardize my reputation.

Stephen drummed his fingers on the bar. "You realize what will happen to us if anyone finds out about us."

"You needn't remind me." I regretted the shortness of my tone, but I didn't need Stephen to remind me of the obvious. Luckily, people only believed in monsters that lurked between the pages of Francis's aforementioned penny dreadfuls, stories which caused as much anxiety among parents as alcohol and gambling amongst temperance groups.

Stephen came up behind me. He draped his arms around my neck, fingers playing with the studs on my shirt. He nipped my earlobe. Not hard enough to draw blood, but enough to cause me to stiffen.

"We need to find Charlotte."

"If that's true, why are we still here?" Stephen's warm breath tickled the side of my face. "I see a perfect opportunity."

He could be persuasive. "If anything happens to her..."

He straightened, and looked at me. "You did everything you could. What matters is us. Not the Ripper, not Charlotte, not any of it. Only you and me."

How could he be so selfish? I started to rise, but he pushed me back onto the bar chair. His mouth pressed against mine in a desperate kiss.

Despite my annoyance, I responded. Part of my mind fought against my rising passion. The thrill of making love here in The Cloak and Dagger warred with the fear of Charlotte lying hurt and dying or, even worse, already dead.

Rough hands pressed against my thighs. Stephen continued to kiss me as if this would be our last time together. Our tongues met, entwining, while he undid my shirt studs and loosened my collar.

We broke the kiss, both now too intent on the bloodlust. I lifted his hand and bit his wrist. Stephen stiffened before leaning down and feeding from his preferred place. My carotid artery pulsed in counterpoint to his heartbeat.

Sated, we released each another. I kissed him, tasting my blood. He pressed his index finger against my mouth, catching a droplet of blood, and brought it to his lips.

"Now what?" he asked.

I turned off the gas lamps. "Good question. I don't know." I'd hoped tonight would give me a clue to Charlotte's whereabouts. I ushered Stephen outside and locked the tavern door.

Above, the crescent moon played hide and seek with low hanging clouds.

The night was eerily silent. Under the glow of gas lamps, we headed home, passing houses with lamps in the window, barriers against monsters of the night.

Monsters like the Ripper. Monsters like us.

Chapter Fifteen

I slept fitfully that morning, listening for the telephone or a knock at the door. All I wanted was to hear Charlotte's voice. If not that, at least a phone call from Francis or Sergeant Pierce telling me she was fine and not to worry. Stephen convinced me that, without a plan, we'd only waste time and energy.

Hearing voices, I leapt out of bed, throwing the covers back. They slid onto the floor, and I nearly tripped over them in my haste to grab my robe.

I fastened the silk belt as I ran downstairs.

Sergeant Pierce and Stephen stood in the living room. The officer held a small package. He looked more serious than normal as he handed it to me.

I lifted the lid, stomach knotting with anticipation and dread.

Ten years ago, the London police had received a similar package. Inside was a kidney and a note, purportedly written by the Ripper, talking about how he'd cooked and eaten the other one, finding it quite delicious.

This time there was no kidney and no note. Just a severed finger with a gold ring, inlaid with an opal stone, whose iridescent surface caught the light of a gas lamp.

I handed the box back to the sergeant.

"When did it arrive?" I asked.

Sergeant Pierce placed his grisly package on the fireplace mantle. "This morning. It was addressed to me."

"You don't think the Ripper knows you're investigating the murders?"

He inclined his head. "It's public knowledge. Question is, what's he trying to tell us?"

"Do you recognize the ring?" I opened the box and stared at the jewel, trying to ignore the grisly remnant it encircled.

Sergeant Pierce studied it, a thoughtful expression on his face. "That Livvie lass was wearing it."

"But why not keep the ring?" Unless the Ripper or Rosie wanted to send a message. Perhaps this was Rosie's way of accusing Olivia of living above her station. Livvie had had dreams and opportunities to pursue them. Rosie, a product of the tenements, had disease, poverty, and the prospect of an early death. Even worse, a good chance she'd become what she hated most.

Sergeant Pierce retrieved his package. "I'll take this back to the station to be analyzed for fingerprints." He tipped his hat. "Good day, Mr. James."

I saw him to the door. "Any news about Charlotte?"

He shook his head. "Nothing yet, but we're not giving up."

"Thank you." I shut the door and returned to the kitchen to find Stephen cooking breakfast.

"What does Sergeant Pierce intend to do?" he asked, breaking eggs into a frying pan.

"I'm not sure." I sat in a chair and closed my eyes, listening to the sizzle of grease popping and spitting. The aroma of bacon enticed me to open my eyes. Part of me was afraid I might see visions of blistered severed fingers.

"I wish we had that ring," Stephen said, using a turner to keep the eggs from burning.

"Why?"

He gave me a meaningful look. "Maybe I've been keeping a secret from you. Call Francis and tell him to go to the police station. Tell him to ask Sergeant Pierce to show him the ring. He'll know what to do." He grinned, his enthusiasm evident.

I'd no idea what he meant, but I complied.

Francis answered the phone by yawning in my ear. "Hello?"

"This is Nathan. I need you to do me a favor."

"What is it, sir?" His voice sounded rough from lack of sleep.

I relayed Stephen's message.

Francis chuckled. "I see. Tell Stephen I'll be happy to oblige."

"Thank you. I appreciate it." I hung up, unsure if I were the only one who didn't get a secret joke.

"Will he do it?" Stephen plated the bacon and eggs.

"Yes, although I wish you would tell me what it is you want him to do." I tried to give him a severe look, but something in Stephen's smug expression only caused me to throw up my hands in frustration. "Fine. Keep your secrets."

"You'll understand." He set a plate before me. "Now eat. That ring isn't going anywhere."

"I've a feeling you and Francis talk more than I thought." I finished breakfast, then went upstairs to dress. On the way downstairs, I stopped in my office and glanced over the piles of notes. I'd a feeling I was almost there, that the proverbial net was hovering over the Ripper's head, and, at any moment, we'd trap him.

The door opened and Stephen stuck his head in. "Are you all right?" He sounded concerned. "I didn't mean to upset you."

I straightened my notes. "You didn't."

He pointed at my desk. "What's that?"

"What?" I turned to see what he was looking at, a daguerreotype of me in my police uniform while in London. Shoved beneath a pile of papers, I hadn't looked at it for years, had forgotten it.

"Oh, that." I handed it to him. "Albertson, the officer who arrested me, gave that to me as a gift when I became a London bobby."

Stephen turned it over. On the back, Albertson had written, "I have faith in you. Good luck!" and signed his name.

"You were close?"

Did I detect a hint of jealousy? I put the print back on the desk. "He was a good friend, but we didn't have a relationship." I didn't add I'd felt like a failure for leaving London and not catching the Ripper. Would Michael forgive me if he were alive?

Stephen said nothing as he left. He returned a few minutes later, and handed me a derringer.

"How long have you had this?" I opened the chambers to find two silver bullets.

He gestured to the elaborate scrollwork on the pistol grip. "It's a family heirloom. I had the bullets specially made. Never been fired, except for a duel in 1870."

I hefted the pistol in my palm. It had a nice balance. "I hope you weren't part of that duel."

He gave me a wicked grin. At least he had won.

"Anyway," Stephen continued, "it's becoming far too dangerous for you not to be armed. These bullets can kill a man as well as a werewolf."

"Thank you." I pocketed the gun. "I'll take good care of it."

He waved a dismissive hand. "Only thing I care about is stopping the Ripper."

"I thought you didn't care about this case."

We went into the living room. Stephen sat in the wing chair and picked up the *Courier-Journal* laying on the coffee table. "I don't, except I'm afraid your involvement may be detrimental to our relationship."

He was right, my determination to catch the Ripper drove me to take risks I might not have otherwise.

I looked at him. His legs were crossed, one arm slung across the back of his chair. The centuries hadn't left their mark on his youthful features. And yet, a certain wisdom lingered under the surface, an understanding borne of experience. I loved him. I couldn't see us not spending eternity together.

The rest of the day passed quietly. A few hours later, Francis called.

"What have you found out?" I asked, curious.

"I have the information I need. But it'll be bit before I can share it with your or Stephen."

"Understood." I scratched my head, unsure of his cryptic message. "Please call as soon as you know something."

"Yes, sir." He disconnected.

"It sounds as if Francis has made some progress," Stephen said, his face hidden behind the newspaper. He sounded pleased.

"I hope so." I stared at the receiver. What had I done? Francis wasn't an investigator. If anything happened to him, I'd never forgive myself.

Chapter Sixteen

Despite my concern about Francis's news, I was again encouraged by the possibility we'd find the Ripper or Rosie and they'd lead me to Charlotte.

I paced the living room, voicing my concerns to Stephen. "At first I thought maybe Rosie wanted to get rid of Charlotte because she was a witness to that altercation with Madge. But why wait this long?"

Stephen flicked lint from his pants. "Why indeed?"

"And if they were going to kill her for being a prostitute, they would've already done so."

"True." He watched me, face expressionless, letting me hypothesize, not judging.

"What do they need her for?"

He considered my question. "Bargaining. Maybe they plan to use her in exchange for something."

"But what?" I'd no idea, and that frustrated me. I could hardly eat and drinking blood held no appeal. It was as if I were waiting for someone to tell me the next step in a plan I'd no control over.

Around midnight, I heard the clop of horses' hooves and the creak of wagon wheels. I looked over at Stephen to see if he'd heard it too. He turned his open book over on his knees and cocked his head, listening, as if trying to discern who'd be coming down the street at this hour.

The wagon came to a stop before our house. I nodded for Stephen to answer the door.

A few minutes later, he ushered in a liveried driver. The man said nothing, merely bowed and gestured for me to follow him.

I started past Stephen. He gripped my arm.

"Do you think it's a good idea?" he asked.

I gave his forearm a reassuring squeeze. "I'll be fine. Besides, this may be the only way to find Charlotte."

He knitted his eyebrows. "I don't like it. It has to be a trap."

I patted the pocket where I'd concealed the derringer. "I'll be careful." If this was the only way I'd find Charlotte and the others, I needed to take that chance.

Stephen started toward the entrance, but the driver glared at him.

"Alone." It was the only word he said.

I gave Stephen a reassuring smile, and followed the driver to the carriage. A young woman sat inside, light from the gas streetlamp reflecting off her black hair.

"Rosie, I assume."

"Detective Inspector James. Thank you for coming." She held out a gloved hand and helped me up next to her.

I kissed the back of her hand. "Pleased to meet you." My stomach churned, a queasiness born of apprehension and disgust. Part of me wanted to pull back in revulsion, but another part of me stared at her, fascinated by the arrogance in her intelligent face. Like her father, she'd proved a cunning adversary. "But I'm no longer a DI."

The driver shook the reins, and the horses, sleek and black, like the carriage, clopped off, heading to a destination that only Rosie and the driver knew.

"So you're the inspector my father told me about. One of Scotland Yard's best." Rosie stared ahead.

"If that were true, your father wouldn't be in a position to kill those women or your family."

Rosie shrugged, drawing her wrap tighter around her shoulders. "He said you were the only one to realize he wasn't like other murderers. But you'd have a hard time convincing others." She smiled smugly at me. "He knows what you did in London, but says it won't do you any good. You don't have the prey instinct we do."

"Then you did inherit his ability."

She shrugged. "It certainly made killing easier."

I watched trees and houses roll past the window as we headed south, away from the city. Questions gnawed at me. "You posted Charlotte's bail."

"A blonde wig, and she didn't recognize me."

"Why'd you kill Madge and Livvie? For being prostitutes? Or did you murder Madge because she said you were going to hell."

Rosie gave a derisive snort. "Seems hypocritical for someone to be working as a whore when they professed to wanting a life in the convent. Such insolence must be punished, don't you think?" She studied her nails. "As for Livvie, she thought she was better than me. I had to punish such impertinence."

Although I appreciated her talking to me, I worried what fate awaited. I pressed my hand against the derringer. Two bullets, one for Rosie and one for the Ripper. But what if the driver attacked me? I decided to continue asking questions, while hoping a plan came to me.

"How'd your father know you were here?"

She tucked booted feet under our seat. "Amelia asked him to come." Her eyes narrowed. "At first, he didn't know the truth. He doted on her, even paid for a tintype of us." She gave me a knowing look. I shuddered. Not only was Rosie capable of murder, but also grave robbing. "He was walking through the tenements when he saw me. I guess it's because we're both shifters that he recognized me."

He must've been looking for victims. Or was he searching for Rosie? Did he have a need to know what'd become of his daughter? I leaned back, pressing my fingers to my forehead, trying to ignore the headache forming there. Perhaps I'd never know all the answers, including the Ripper's true identity, and I doubted Rosie would tell me.

"But why murder prostitutes?" I declined to mention her brief foray into that life, sensing if I did, I might not leave the carriage alive. "Sometimes circumstances aren't kind, and people have no choice in what they do."

She stiffened. "Father says it's our job to eliminate those who are impure, imperfect."

"Even your mother and brother?"

She gave me a sidelong glance. "They were mercy killings. I offered Robert a chance to come with us, but he refused. Mother didn't want to understand. When I couldn't make her see our way, Father and I had no choice."

We rode in silence for several minutes. The city gave way to fields and woods. In the distance, wisps of smoke rose from the chimneys of scattered farm houses.

At last, we turned down a dirt trail and pulled up to a one-room tin-and-wood shack. Was Charlotte here?

The driver disembarked first. He helped Rosie down. Before I could follow, he held up a warning hand.

"Hold up your arms."

I obeyed and he frisked me. As his hands got closer to my coat pocket, I tensed.

He gave me a piercing look and grinned. I bit my lower lip as his hand dipped into my pocket and he pulled out the derringer.

"Well, well. What do we have here?" He removed the silver bullets and tossed them into the air. They arced high and disappeared in the overgrowth.

He sneered. "Silver bullets. How quaint."

"The gun's no use to anyone now. Give it back." I held out my hand. "There's no reason for you to keep it." I gave what I hoped was an ingratiating smile.

Instead, the driver slipped Stephen's derringer into his pocket. "Just in case you have more silver bullets on you that I missed." He started toward the cabin, gesturing me to follow.

The interior was bare, dirt floor covered with straw and dirty blankets. A pitcher and basin, both filled with stagnant water, sat in a corner.

A moan caught my attention, and I turned to see a pile of rags stirring. Haunted eyes looked up at me from a gaunt face, and I stumbled back, nausea roiling in my stomach.

Charlotte was barely recognizable. Her head had been shaved, and guttural moans issued from her scarred throat. A foul stench emanated from her.

Livid, I reeled on Rosie. "What've you done to her?"

The Ripper's daughter shrugged. "Nothing she didn't deserve."

I stared at her, trying to understand. "Deserve? What did she do to you?"

Rosie glanced at Charlotte, and wrinkled her nose in disgust. "She's a whore." She looked at me. "How can you be friends with a whore?"

"What do you want?" I dreaded her answer.

She gave me a cruel smile. "Give her your blood. Turn her into a vampire."

My heart trip hammered against my ribs. "She'll die."

Rosie shrugged, wrap slipping from her shoulders. "I'll reveal the truth about you if you don't kill her. How do you think your customers will feel when they hear you're a bloodsucker or worse?" She leaned against the wall, and folded her arms across her chest. "You think we don't know about you or your manservant? Would be a shame if Sergeant Pierce found out, wouldn't it?"

Pain stabbed my solar plexus, and I doubled over, wanting to vomit. "How long have you known?"

Rosie's laugh chilled the air. "Father knew from the beginning. He has spies. But when you left, he'd no idea you came here. Finding you again was a happy coincidence." She paced the floor, dust rising from her steps. "He did some research and learned if one of you died, so would the other." She stopped and cocked her head. "Stephen may have told you if you drank someone's blood, you'd kill them. Did he also tell you that you'd die, too?"

"No." The stench and words made my head reel. Even worse, this talk of blood triggered a desire in me, and I couldn't help but glance at Charlotte. Despite Stephen's warning, I could feel my fangs wanting to drop. Stephen had warned me such bloodlust wasn't uncommon, especially among new vampires. I wasn't immune to such cravings.

"You won't be able to resist. Without your lover, the bloodlust will only become stronger, until it's insatiable." Rosie leaned against the wall. "You could drink my blood, but then you'll die, and so will your lover. What will Charlotte do then? To be honest, she'll never be able to work as a whore. The drugs have damaged her, made her an imbecile." She shrugged. "Maybe she can find work as a scullery maid."

I sank to the floor, sickened. How could I tell Francis about Charlotte? Would he forgive me? And the thought of being responsible for Stephen's death... "I never expected it to turn out this way."

"You tried to destroy my father. You're only getting what you deserve."

Charlotte moaned. Rosie strode toward me, fists clenched. She grabbed my chin, and tilted my jaw. "Go on then. We haven't all day."

I grimaced and tried to pull away, but her grip was an iron vise. She hoisted me off the floor with a strength I'd never imagined and threw me into Charlotte. I thudded against the wall. My knee struck Charlotte's side as I tripped over her, entangling my arms and legs in her dirty skirts.

"Drink her blood!" Rosie screamed. Her blue-gray eyes turned amber, burning with an intense heat, fueled by rage.

I pulled Charlotte into my arms. Her head lolled against my shoulder, neck arched and throat pale. Her carotid artery pulsed, and I smelled her blood, a coppery scent, like old pennies.

Desire spiraled through me and my fangs dropped. Charlotte blinked open bleary eyes, arms snaking up to encircle my neck. There was no recognition in her eyes. The Charlotte I remembered no longer existed. Instead, all that remained was an empty shell and a disturbing childlike innocence. Whatever drugs Rosie had fed Charlotte had reduced her to nothing more than a newborn, devoid of any intelligence or free will.

I turned away, guilt dampening any bloodlust. What kind of life was this? Would it be better to kill her, knowing she'd never recover? I could only hope Francis and Stephen forgave me.

Rosie smirked, obviously enjoying my dilemma. "You haven't much time."

Charlotte started thrashing beneath me, chest heaving, breathing labored. What kind of poison was this?

I pulled her closer, ignoring the foul smell. Speaking in soft, soothing tones, I brushed her hair back from her forehead. Her breasts pushed against my chest, heart fluttering madly.

"It's all right." I closed my eyes, forcing back the tears. "Everything will be all right."

Charlotte tried to talk, but could only manage a weak mewl.

"Don't talk." I pressed my face into her neck, breathing in sweat, old perfume and the overpowering, enticing smell of blood. "I'm sorry. Please, forgive me."

I bit her carotid artery.

Charlotte's eyes flew open. Her back arched. For several minutes her body convulsed, and I gripped her, holding her tight, tears filling my eyes.

A few minutes later, a rush of air escaped her slack mouth. She slipped down, her lifeless body heavy against me.

I'd nothing left. If I were going to die, then I'd kill Rosie, too.

I lunged for her. Rosie sidestepped, a mocking smile on her face. The wall came up fast. I slid a few feet, shoes trying to make purchase on the moldy hay. Knees bent, I pivoted. I found myself facing the carriage driver. Face red, he bellowed. He rushed me, a wooden stake upraised in his right hand. Like Rosie, I stepped to the side. The driver's momentum carried him past me. But his coordination proved worse than mine. He slipped backwards on the ubiquitous hay, landing with a loud thud on his back. The stake fell from his grasp. I leapt to grab it. He tried to turn his body, but all he managed was a groan, breath knocked out of him.

Both Rosie and I dived for the stake. I jammed my elbow into her side, knocking her off balance. Rosie cursed, and tackled me. I pinned her arms. I brought us crashing to the floor. I hit the ground and rolled, immediately using my knees to throw her off me. She rolled. She sprang up on all fours, eyes focused on me, breath coming in short pants.

I couldn't take my eyes off either one of them. The driver moaned and tried to sit up, his movements shaky. He rolled to his side, baleful eyes focused on me.

Rosie dived past me, skirts rustling. Her triumphant cry broke into another curse as I grabbed her by the leg. I hauled her back, not caring if I was manhandling her or not.

"You're not getting that stake," I said.

I'd never seen a mythological harpy in real life, but Rosie's expression seemed to imitate one quite well. Her eyes narrowed, mouth open in a silent, angry scream. I pushed her aside and ran toward the stake, snatching it up with one hand.

"Get it!" Rosie screamed at the driver.

His steps were slower than normal, perhaps a result of his fall. He grinned at me, cracking his knuckles. His hand slipped into his pocket. He pulled out a nasty-looking rusty blade.

If I backed away, I'd end up against the wall, and in a bad position. I glanced at Rosie. She stood, arms akimbo, that smug look on her face. Part of me relished the idea of slapping her, this unrepentant, murdering wench, not for what she'd threatened to do to me, but for what atrocities she'd done to Charlotte.

I jammed the stake between my teeth, taking care to avoid splinters. By itself, the weapon proved useless, another stick of wood. Only when it pierced my heart, would it be lethal. I'd no intention of being stabbed.

Yanking off my jacket, I ran at the driver and pushed my coat over his head and face, pushing him backwards. His hand swung wildly, blade slicing the air. A well-aimed foot, and the knife flew across the room. It hit the wall, and dropped to the wood floor with a clatter.

Before Rosie's driver could push my coat off, I plunged the sharp tip of the stake into his heart. Blood spurted in a macabre fountain, ruining his pristine uniform. Satisfied he was either dead, or close to it, I pulled the bloody stake free, and snapped it in half. Charlotte's blood had invigorated me, but for how long?

Rosie stared, eyes wide with shock, at her lifeless driver. "Damn you!" She charged, fingernails aimed at my face.

I lashed out with my arm, knocking her aside. She stumbled into the wall, falling in a heap.

Breathing labored, I clenched my fists. "Get up." Bloodlust spiraled through me, fueled by an urge to rip open her throat and let blood gush from her arteries.

Rosie growled, a low, warning sound. She turned, eyes burning red. Her tongue slipped from between her lips, and she gave me a malevolent smile.

Watching Rosie transform proved more difficult to watch than examining the mangled corpses, but I couldn't look away. She fell to her hands and knees, and made a keening noise. I winched as her bones crunched and tore as they lengthened and shortened. Rosie's head fell back. She clawed the air, pain raking her face. She grabbed her skirt and blouse. She ripped off her clothes from her body, flinging them aside. Black fur spurted in patches over her thin body. She growled again, mouth and jaw elongating, teeth growing into sharp points.

We stared at each other. Rosie may have become a wolf shifter, but the eyes staring at me held human intelligence.

She jumped, powerful hindquarters propelling her through the air.

I dodged. She hit the floor, skittering into the wall, claws scrabbling at the wood.

My moment of triumph lasted only a few seconds. I reeled, vision blurring, and barely had time to register a blur of black fur above me. I tried to run, but my legs refused to move, body slogging as if through a field of pitch.

Something hit my back, knocking me forward. I hit the floor with a whoosh, breath burning in my lungs. A sharp pain raked across my back and panic seized me. What was happening? Was I dying? I twisted, trying to throw the heavy weight off, but my body refused to move, mocking my efforts.

Through a wavering haze, I looked up, unable to comprehend what I saw, and yet understanding it was a wolf. No, not a wolf. Rosie. Forepaws planted on my chest, she leaned down, hot saliva dripping on my neck.

I stared into a mouthful of fangs and swallowed hard. Adrenaline raced through my blood. My energy level had plummeted. I pushed against her broad, muscular chest, hoping to throw her off, but her weight and strength surpassed mine, and sharp claws sought purchase in my flesh.

I screamed, body writhing with pain. The coppery smell of blood filled my nose, my blood. Rage and fear fought within me, fueled by a desire to kill Rosie. I needed to escape this corpse-infested hovel.

My world faded into a myriad of shimmering colors. I gazed, entranced, unable to look away.

A loud crack, then a mangled yelp.

My arms reached heavenward, trying to stop my beautiful aurora borealis from leaving. But the weakened muscles refused to cooperate, and my arms fell to my sides, useless appendages.

How strange and wonderful this afterlife seemed...

***

How long I laid there, I'd no idea. Through a wispy fog, someone called my name. Blinking open heavy eyelids, I tried to move, but couldn't. My eyes closed again, heavy with fatigue. I struggled for breath, lungs burning.

Someone pressed a hand on my chest. Panicked, I started to thrash, but someone spoke in a soothing voice. "Take a deep breath."

I allowed myself to respond. The heaviness abated, and the strange haze melted.

"That's it. Relax."

Stephen's voice. No, that couldn't be right. He didn't know I was here.

"Is he all right?"

Francis? Perhaps memories were filtering their way through my subconscious as my life force ebbed. To die, surrounded by my lover and friend, warmed me, and I smiled.

"I don't think so."

Someone slapped my face. I winced, eyes still closed. I didn't want to see the carnage. I wanted to die remembering my lovely borealis.

"He's reacted!"

"That hurt!" My words came out slurred, but I relished them. I took a couple deep breaths, then opened my eyes.

A face swam before me. Sapphire eyes set in a saturnine face, framed by long black hair.

"S-Stephen?" I curled my hand around his wrist.

"Nathan!" Stephen grabbed me in a tight hug, nearly cutting off my breath. "We thought we'd lost you."

I struggled out of his grasp, curious to see what'd happened. Looking around, I saw Rosie's body, still in wolf form. She lay on her side, blood trailing from the bullet wound in her neck.

Francis leaned in the doorway. He held a revolver.

I stared at him. Milquetoast, skinny Francis?

The derringer. I sagged against Stephen, grasping his shirt, as if trying to assure myself he stood next to me. Words caught in my throat. "I'm sorry. Your gun..."

"We'll find it." He wiped my hair from my forehead. "Your body's had an awful shock. You've been poisoned."

"I know. Charlotte. Rosie poisoned her." I hoped my words made sense. "She forced me to drink Charlotte's blood." I gave Francis a beseeching look. "I'm sorry, Francis. But her mind was destroyed. There was nothing I could do."

He nodded, but from the distant expression on his face, I feared he didn't believe me. Had I ruined our friendship? Regret filled me, and I turned away, sickened. Would he consider me a monster, refuse to have anything to do with me or Stephen?

Stephen shook his head. "I meant blood poisoning. That's why you can't drink anyone else's but mine. Her blood was poisonous to you."

I paled, but not because of that revelation. Stephen had just confessed to us being vampires in front of Francis. Mortified, I glanced at him, hoping he hadn't heard.

To my surprise, Francis smiled. "Did you think I didn't know? Stephen and I are old friends. He asked me to move here and work for you."

"How did you find me?" It was an effort to speak, and I struggled to remain conscious. I took a few deep breaths, lungs searing with pain. Looking down, I stared at the slash marks marred by dried blood. Rosie's claws had rendered my flesh to ribbons. Somehow, the blood poison had acted as an anesthesia. I shuddered. If Stephen and Francis hadn't shown when they had, I probably would've been mauled to death and not even realized it.

Stephen wiped my fevered brow with his handkerchief. "We're bonded. I'll find you wherever you are."

"What about the Ripper?" My mouth was dry and I swallowed what saliva I could. I needed water, but I wouldn't drink that filth in the basin.

"He won't be coming back unless werewolves are immortal," Francis said.

"Remember that ring?" Stephen asked.

I nodded, not comprehending, but not wanting to seem ignorant.

Francis gave me a wicked smile. "With the ring, I was able to pick up the Ripper and Rosie's scents. I guess they didn't realize there was another shifter in the city."

I stared at him, fascinated. "That's why Stephen wanted you to come with us." My lover had known all along we might need Francis's help.

I turned to Stephen. "What happened to the Ripper?"

"We chased him through the streets. Someone heard the commotion, and called the police. He tried to escape across the railway bridge, but Sergeant Pierce shot him. They're searching for his body in the Ohio River."

"Will they know it's the Ripper when they recover him?"

"Probably not, but what matters is he'll no longer be a threat." Francis squeezed my shoulder. "Don't blame yourself for what happened to Charlotte. You did what you had to do."

I grasped his hand. "I know how much you cared about her." It was the first time I'd acknowledged his relationship with Charlotte. "I'm sorry I couldn't save her."

Francis gripped my hand for a second, then released me. He walked to where Charlotte lied and made the sign of the cross over her body. He lifted Charlotte in his arms and started for the door. "Let's go home."

"What about Rosie and the driver?"

Stephen gave the corpses a disdainful look. "Let them rot here."

I started to walk, but my legs trembled with each step. How long would it take for the poison to wear off?

Somehow, leaning on Stephen, I made it to the door, muscles sore and protesting. Francis laid Charlotte in the back of a wagon. Two drays snorted and pawed the dirt. The black carriage and horses had vanished. I suspected Stephen and Francis had released them.

"Ready?" Francis hopped on the buckboard and shook the reins.

The horses neighed, bodies swaying in their braces. Francis clucked at them and they moved forward. My stomach lurched as the wagon rattled over the underbrush.

Stephen reached for my hand and squeezed it. I pressed back, tired but happy. Leaning my head against his shoulder, I closed my eyes.

"Rest in peace, Grace and Charlotte."

About the Author

Pamela Turner drinks too much coffee, and wishes she could write perfect first drafts. Publications include reviews, articles, poetry, and short fiction. Her 10-minute play, "Brides of Deceit," was part of a local performance, and "Cemetery" placed second in The Writers Place short/teleplay screenplay competition. Other publications include the urban fantasy/ paranormal short novels, *Death Sword* and *Exterminating Angel* (Spring 2014), both from Lyrical Press/Kensington Publishing Corp. Short dark fiction stories include the upcoming "Gabrielle" (Hekate Press) and "Family Tradition" (MuseItUp Publishing), a finalist in the EPIC 2014 EBook Awards. She's a member of RWA, Sisters in Crime, EPIC, and a supporting member of HWA. Besides coffee, she likes cats, cemeteries, and old abandoned buildings. You can find her at *www.pamelaturner.net*

SEASONS OF DEATH

THE SMOKY MOUNTAINS MURDERS
by Marlene Mitchell, Gary Yeagle

In 1969 in the mountains of eastern Tennessee, a poor backwoods farmer and his wife were brutally shot and killed by four drunken hunters, along with their three dogs, horse and two fawns. The farmer's two young sons managed to escape but were unable to identify the killers. Now decades later, someone has decided to take revenge.
[Murder Mystery, ages 14+]

GEMINI'S WAR
Gemini Rising, Book One
by Amy McCorkle

Gemini is hunted by her gangster father for escaping the sexual slavery that she'd been sold into. Along the way, she falls in love with a British rogue operative. This first book in Gemini's trilogy is a great read for fans of James Bond and The Girl with the Dragon Tattoo.
[Women's Adventure, ages 14+]